UNLEASHED

KARL HILL

BLOODHOUND
— BOOKS —

Print ISBN 978-1-913419-70-7

1

Attack is the best form of defence. Assisted by skill, cunning, and a whole lot of fucking luck.
Advice given to new recruits of the 22nd Special Air Service Regiment.

The weather didn't matter. Not to Adam Black. Snow, hail, fog. Like clockwork, he went for his evening run. Whether it was habit or instinct or even enjoyment, he couldn't be sure. Maybe insanity. But it was ingrained, second nature, down to the harshest training known to man, and so this particular evening was no different from any other. Except the moon. It was a blood moon, unobscured by cloud, surrounded by a million stars.

"Unlucky," Jennifer predicted, as she watched him tying up his trainers, a half smile playing on her lips.

"Or maybe lucky." Black laughed. "While I'm out, your lottery ticket might come up."

"Which would be nice, if I ever bought one."

"A major flaw. Let's be honest. Having all that money would

be… let me think. Boring? Who wants to be filthy rich, and live a life of shameful decadence and incredible luxury? Surely not you."

Jennifer ruffled his hair. "Of course not. Heaven forbid. I can barely imagine how awful it would be. Dinner's going to be ready in half an hour. If you're late, you're looking at soggy pasta."

Black grinned.

"Half an hour or soggy pasta. Put that on my headstone, please."

"I'd rather you put this on your head." She handed him a black woollen mountain hat. "It's minus two."

Black regarded the hat with scepticism. "Seriously?"

"Seriously. I don't want any husband of mine wandering about with frostbitten ears. Embarrassing. For me, that is. What would the neighbours say?"

He shrugged – it was no use arguing – and put it on. Even with the hat, he cut a compelling figure. Unobtrusively muscular, handsome in a hard-bitten way, rather harsh cheekbones, dark eyes.

"Tough guys shouldn't need to wear hats like this."

"Which is precisely why you need to wear one. See you in half an hour, tough guy. Clock's ticking."

2

Black closed the front door behind him; it felt colder than minus two, coming immediately from the warmth. His skin tingled; his lungs felt the bite of the crisp air. A wisp of cloud formed with every breath.

He was dressed for the occasion; close-fitting long-sleeved vest under a light sweat-top with high-viz reflective bands; cycling shorts under semi-loose track bottoms; ankle socks; padded cycling gloves. And the hat, of course. He had tried wearing flat-soled running shoes – if ancient man got around on his bare soles, then why couldn't trendy modern man? Plus, the running magazines raved about the concept. Black had tried them for six months, eventually judging the idea as bullshit. Too much stress on the ankles, the calves, his feet sensing every miniscule stone, every edge, every crack. The running magazines were consigned to the bin. Back to the traditional running shoe, all cushioned and springy.

He loosened up for a few seconds in the front garden. He avoided stretching – it was overrated, increasing the odds of a pulled muscle. Instead, he jumped gently on the spot, shaking his arms, rotating his neck, swivelling his shoulders, breathing deeply, filling his lungs.

He looked up at the night sky, and there it was. A blood moon. A strange, dusky-red circle, out of place amongst the stars. Like a perfect gemstone. Almost alien. He had seen more blood than he cared to remember and knew its every shade, every permutation. This was the colour of old blood, he decided. Blood that leaves a stain. Blood that doesn't wash away.

He began his run. His programme changed every week. To keep rigidly to the same route was recipe for disaster – the mind became bored, jaded, affecting the body's performance, until running became worse than a chore, an ordeal.

This particular week it was twice around the village park. From their cottage and back again, it was about a four-and-a-half-mile run. They lived a mile from the village of Eaglesham, located on the outskirts of Glasgow. A village set on the incline of a hill, in the broad shape of a capital A, structured round a common green. An eighteenth century 'planned village', filled to the brim with listed buildings, cute cottages, secret lanes. Created that way by the Earl of Eglinton, a rich Scottish aristocrat, apparently an altruist in his day. A cotton mill once stood in the centre, employing upwards of two hundred people. The cotton industry died, the mill died with it, reduced to a scattering of stones. The remnants could still be found, if a person looked hard enough, amongst the trees and bushes and long grass. Black was never a history buff. He had never bothered looking, and never would.

The hill going up to the apex of the A was steep, a half mile of slog. Going down was a breeze, though the road treacherous with ice; a twisted ankle was not unknown.

He passed the darkness of woodland, separated from the pavement by a low dry-stone wall, until he reached the first streetlight, and then houses on either side of a two-lane road. He got to the centre of the village – a row of small, flat-roofed shops – then turned to his right and began the ascent. Here, the road was narrow, the pavement barely wide enough for one person. On his right shoulder were rows of tall, squeezed, terraced houses with crow-stepped gables, once homes for the mill workers, now overpriced getaway dwellings for rich people with money to burn, and time to do it. On his left, the park, a blot of deep shadow. He slowed a little; the incline was steep. He passed windows and glimpsed people doing what they do, going about their lives: watching TV; cooking dinner; sitting at a table; kids doing homework. Routine stuff. Normal stuff.

Halfway up, and he got to the only pub in Eaglesham, the Old Swan. A building of buff-red sandstone, Georgian windows, black-painted sills. People were outside in the freezing cold, smoking, chatting, maybe a half dozen. It was noisy inside – a week before Christmas. Party time.

He veered onto the road to avoid any collisions. Someone shouted something. A man's voice. Black's ears were muffled by his hat. What was it? Two words. *Fucking clown*. Could be. Black ignored him, ran on, and in a few seconds was beyond the pub, and back to running past more houses. His route would take him a second time by the Old Swan. By then, whoever had shouted would be finished his smoke and back inside sinking pints.

Probably.

Black couldn't have been more wrong.

3

Damian Grant was in a crazy shit mood, and when he was like that, crazy shit tended to happen. His cousin, and boyhood friend Tommy 'Teacup' Thomson, had seen this played out a hundred times before, and though he'd always gone along with it, mostly because he was paid to do so, he still never liked it. Teacup was no stranger to violence himself – professional boxer turned enforcer and all-round fixer – but Damian cranked it up to a whole new level.

Teacup was watching Damian, in the process of snorting his third line of cocaine from a glass-topped side table. They were not the only people in the room. Sitting in an armchair by a bay window, reading a newspaper and seemingly oblivious to Damian's rants, was William Blakely. Contracted up from Manchester. Dressed impeccably as ever: powder-blue woollen suit, crisp white shirt, white silk tie, shoes polished until they gleamed like mirrors, silver cufflinks. What people didn't know, was that he carried a knuckleduster in one inside pocket, and a blade tucked in the other. And he wasn't scared to use them.

But Damian Grant was in a crazy shit mood, and Teacup didn't know how the hell the day was going to pan out.

"I so needed that." Damian sighed, reclining back on a beige leather chair, legs sprawled in front of him, two pale limbs sticking out like matchsticks from a velvet bathrobe. "I know you disapprove, but guess what. I couldn't care less. Your disapproval gives me no concern. Do you know why?"

"Why?"

"Because, old friend, with the crap I've to put up with, no fucking wonder I take sanctuary in hard drugs. Do you like that word, Teacup?"

"What word?"

"Sanctuary. That's what this shit gives me. Sheer fucking sanctuary. Sanctuary from the old bastard."

Teacup paused, thoughtful. He had to be careful what he said. Every word was important, when Damian was like this. Every word had consequences. On the one hand, the son. On the other, the father. A balancing act. He had to be loyal to both. If word got back he'd spoken ill of Mr Grant, then he'd have a problem. Consequences.

"Your father's not an easy man," Teacup replied, nodding sagely, as if in agreement. "He can be difficult. But then, he's got a lot on his plate."

"A lot on his plate!" Damian glared at him, eyes shining. "What does that even mean! If you're going to open your mouth, at least try to talk some sense!" Damian's voice took an icy tone. "It's about respect. Or lack of. I'm not a fucking errand boy. Do this! Do that! He snaps his fingers and I come running. Scurrying about like his fucking pet dog. Let me explain something to you. Come close."

Damian leaned forward in his chair. Teacup, sitting opposite, bent closer.

"It's destroying me," Damian said, his voice low, barely a whisper. "It's ripping out my fucking soul." He clutched his hand to his chest, in mock drama. "You understand this?"

He stared at Teacup. Teacup could only stare back.

"When all's said and done," Damian continued softly, "I'm quite entitled to my little dalliances." He raised his head back and burst out laughing – a raw, wild sound. "What do you think of that word, Mr Blakely?"

William Blakely looked up from his newspaper. He spoke in a quiet, measured tone, at odds with his close-cropped haircut and heavy, blunt features.

"What word was that?"

"Dalliances! Fucking *dalliances!* Awesome, don't you think?"

Blakely smiled. "Now there speaks an educated man," he said, and resumed reading his newspaper.

And Teacup agreed. No expense had been spared in Damian Grant's education. Private schooling (though he had been expelled from two schools), private tuition. He should have done better but hadn't. His father, Peter Grant, never got the chance to get an education, had clawed his way up from the street, and so had lavished on his son everything money could buy. Only natural, a father looking out for his son, Teacup thought. But Damian had spat it back in his father's face. Big time. It was difficult not to hear the bitterness from his voice when he spoke.

"That's your third line today, Damian. Can I make a suggestion?"

"Watch out! Teacup's about to make a suggestion. This should be something."

Teacup licked his lips. *What the hell,* he thought.

"A night in wouldn't do any harm."

Silence. Damian regarded him with a long, thoughtful stare. Then he spoke, his tone quiet, almost reasonable. Not a good sign.

"A night in? Really? That's your suggestion?"

Teacup didn't respond. He'd said the wrong thing, and knew it.

"Who do you think you're talking to?" said Damian. Another silence. William Blakely looked up from his newspaper for a second time. Suddenly, Teacup heard a sound – the beat of his own heart.

"I'm not a fucking three-year-old," said Damian softly. "Don't condescend to me, Teacup, or I swear, you're out on your arse – and then what would Daddy say. One word from me, and he'd have your fucking guts. He'd string you up by the fucking balls!"

Which was true, reflected Teacup. The simple fact was, despite being family, he was on the payroll, as was William Blakely, who had been brought up from Manchester specially. And they were getting paid to do a most specific job; babysit Damian during the Christmas period, when Damian was capable of the craziest shit. If Teacup left Damian's side, for any reason, then he was in trouble. And Damian had been hitting the drugs and booze extra hard for a week, causing mayhem in every club, every pub. Nowhere was safe. *Sanctuary,* thought Teacup. There was none. Damian Grant had the stamina of a horse, and a strong inclination towards extreme violence. A difficult mix to handle, for anyone.

And then Teacup had an idea. He raised both his hands in placation. "No offence meant, Damian. I get concerned for you. You know that. Why don't we try something different tonight?"

"Another of Teacup's suggestions. This had better be an improvement on the last one."

Teacup hoped it was. "We've been to every bar and club in Glasgow. Let's go somewhere different. Somewhere a bit..." Teacup had to scrape around for the right words. "...out of the way. A change of scenery. Somewhere not so noisy. Somewhere... unusual."

Damian brushed away white powder from beneath his nose, scrutinising Teacup with slit eyes.

"Unusual? Out of the way?" He sniffed. "I like the sound of

that. Maybe a change of scenery is what we need." He sat back. "This has potential. Maybe. Do you like that word, Mr Blakely? *Potential!*"

"Love it," responded Blakely in a dry voice. It was obvious he didn't give a shit.

"Do you have anywhere in mind?" asked Damian.

Teacup nodded. A place conjured up from old memories.

"Actually, I do. A country pub, where the beer's good, and cheap, and no one's going to bother us. Remote. No aggravation. I was there years ago. We can relax, have a laugh. Chill out. Maybe like old times. What do you think?"

Damian pursed his lips.

"Like old times? What the fuck does that mean?" His face broke into a grin. "A country pub? For starters, I hate the country. Full of cow crap and horse's piss, and fuck knows what else. What if you need to shit? What do we do then? Squat over some hole in some field in the middle of the fucking snow? What about pussy? I'm not about to shag some stray sheep. A lot of questions, Teacup."

"I would never crap in a field, personally," interrupted Blakely. "We would never do that in Manchester. No chance. We've got style, you understand. The stray sheep however… that's more tempting. What word was it you used – potential? That would have real potential. If I'm lucky, that is." He gave a steely smile. "Better wear my best shirt. And change my underpants."

Everyone laughed. Teacup gave a silent sigh of relief. The tension was broken. For now. And if he could coax Damian to a place where there were no other mad bastards, then they just might survive an evening unscathed. Maybe. It was a big ask.

Damian jumped to his feet, already buzzing with the effects of the cocaine. Teacup knew the routine. He watched silently as Damian padded through to the open-plan kitchen and fixed himself a tall vodka from a large array of bottles on the worktop, which he gulped down in one.

"I can't tempt you?" Damian asked, gesturing to Blakely.

Blakely looked over, smiled, waved his hand in the negative. "On duty, you understand."

"That's right," said Damian, giving a mock salute. "On duty, Mr Blakely! You need to keep that co-ordination of yours in tip-top condition when the old knuckleduster comes out of his resting home, to wreak havoc and devastation." Damian cocked his head to one side. "The truth is, I've never seen someone use a knuckleduster before. Must do a bit of real damage to a man's face. Or a woman's, for that matter."

"It can do," chuckled Blakely. "Untold damage. Caves the bones in, and the face implodes. Folds in on itself. Can rip a nose right off. Blinded a man once. The eye just popped out, like a fucking snooker ball. Bad news for most people. But for your average Glaswegian, it's like a face improvement. I say that only because the average Glaswegian I've met, present company excluded, is the ugliest bastard in the western hemisphere."

"Too true!" Damian laughed as he poured himself another large tumbler of neat vodka.

"But the blade is different," continued Blakely, his voice quiet and sombre. "The blade isn't showy. There's no..." Blakely's brow creased as he struggled for the right expression. "... *theatre,* if you catch my meaning. It doesn't maim or disfigure, unless it's just a message you're sending. The blade is honest. It's clean. Done right, puncture the heart, and it's over. Goodnight Vienna. You can't argue with a blade. Does the job fucking proper."

"Fuck me!" Damian waved his drink about, splashing it on the kitchen worktop. "This man is a fucking philosopher. Hats off to Mr Blakely. What do you think, Teacup? Knuckleduster or blade?"

Teacup frowned. It was such a ridiculous question. But he had to go through the motions.

"Neither. Way too personal. How about a double-barrelled shotgun? Sawn off, for maximum impact. No shitting about, instant head explosion. All done from a safe distance. Job complete. And no blood on your flash Gucci shoes."

Damian gave a wild burst of high-pitched laughter. "We're going to party tonight, boys!"

He downed the remnants of his vodka, grabbed a bottle, and lurched out of the kitchen, and the lounge, making his way to his bedroom at the end of the hall, singing as he went. He would shower, change, polish off more vodka, and undoubtedly snort more cocaine up his nasal passages. Teacup was used to the routine and dreaded it.

Blakely glanced at him, shrugged, and focused back onto the newspaper. "Good idea."

"What?"

"A country pub. Quick thinking. Could mean less trouble, if we handle it right. Keep him off the spirits. And any more drugs, if we can."

"If we can." Teacup got to his feet and made his way to the bay window beside Blakely. The penthouse flat they were in was a gift from Damian's father, to his only son, and must have cost a cool half a million. Possibly more. And one thing was certain – you got a good view for your money. Teacup gazed at the scenery – in the near distance, a cluttered landscape of rooftops and chimneys, and beyond, roads and bridges, and the broad river Clyde, and in the far distance, hills the colour of pale grey under the dreary winter sun. Somewhere nestled in those hills was their destination tonight. And tonight was supposed to be a blood moon, he had heard.

He prayed to Christ that's where the blood stayed.

4

Black glanced up at the sky; the moon held centre stage, like a perfect pebble in a glittering black desert. He had completed the first lap. He was at the foot of the A, where it was flat. He'd found a second wind. The next lap would be easier, he knew. No niggles, no aches. Feeling good. The chill had gone; his muscles were loose and easy. He could run for a hundred miles. He increased his pace, thinking of the wonderfully described *soggy pasta* his wife had threatened him with, if he were late. He reached the turning point and made his way up the hill again. The glow from the street lights gave a strange, witchy quality to the houses and pavement, as if he were running through another world, in another time. Running through a dream. He wondered briefly if he would encounter any more insults at the pub, a half mile up the road. The air was still, and calm.

Perfect, he thought.

~

They arrived at 5pm.

Teacup knew about the Old Swan because he'd been there

once, years back, with his father, and had vague memories of a quiet, sedate atmosphere, where one or two locals sat nursing pints and chatted in low voices. His father had landed a job fixing a roof for someone who lived in the village, and Teacup had helped as a boy, carrying slates up and down a ladder, as he recalled. That was long ago. His dad was long dead, lungs shrivelled black with cancer. Teacup had never been on a roof since, and never intended to again.

They parked the Range Rover a short walk from the pub, only forty yards from the door. Still Damian managed to complain.

"Fucking hillbillies better not key the car," he grumbled.

"Don't panic. No one's going to key the car," said Teacup.

Damian didn't let up. "This is a fucking mountain climb. You could have told me we were going on a hike. Would have brought my climbing boots."

"You don't have climbing boots, Damian," said Teacup.

"This is the country." William Blakely was walking beside him, taking an exaggerated breath. "Smell that country air. Take it in, boys. Clears the lungs. Better than all that city shit."

"Just look out for cow shit." Damian laughed, perhaps a little too loudly, and they all laughed together. So far so good, thought Teacup. Damian was laughing, a good sign. It could all change in a split second.

The pub was warm and friendly, and fuller than Teacup had expected, with people out for pre-Christmas party drinks. A warm-up before fun time in the city, he realised. It was *Olde Worlde*. A real log fire crackled in a brown stone hearth, oak beams blackened with age and smoke ran the length of a low ceiling; the floor was simple dark wood, which creaked with every step; the walls were simple stone the colour of cream, with pictures of faded places and faces. High stools lined the bar; people laughed and chatted in wooden booths and round rough-hewn wooden tables.

They got three stools at the bar.

"What are you having, boys?" Damian was still buzzing. His eyes sparkled. When he spoke, the words rattled out, tripping over each other. "No – let me guess. Mr Blakely – you'll be wanting a diet Coke with a slice of orange. Or was it lemon? Teacup – you'll be having some woman's drink. Fresh blackcurrant juice and lemonade. Or some other piss. Or let me guess! Maybe a cup of fine Darjeeling tea, in a fine china teacup, for the man they call Mr Tommy 'Teacup' Thomson."

"Blackcurrant and lemonade is as strong as it gets." Teacup shrugged. "Orders are orders."

He knew instantly, as soon as the words left his mouth, that he'd said the wrong thing.

"Orders are orders?" repeated Damian. "That's the response I get? My dad's wee wooden clockwork soldier?"

He leaned forward, an inch from Teacup's ear, and spoke in a rasping whisper. "Orders are orders. Then get the orders in. And you can pay for them too. Mine's a double. Whisky. Any fucking type. And a pint. Please. Pretty please."

He stared at Teacup, close up, and stayed that way for several long uncomfortable seconds. Teacup tensed, aware anything could happen. He didn't reply. He didn't twitch a muscle. He was a friend, he was a relative. But when Damian Grant was in the zone, no one was safe.

Damian suddenly laughed, and pinched Teacup's cheek. "I'm only joshing, you silly prick." He pulled out a wallet from the zip pocket of his leather jacket, and fished out a fifty-pound note, which he slapped on the bar. "Take it from that. Back in a mo." He manoeuvred himself off the high stool and made his way to the gents' toilet.

Blakely blew through his lips. "He's off for another score."

Teacup nodded. "That'll be his fifth today. Maybe more. You lose count. And I thought this would be easy. Better brace yourself. Could be a long night."

Blakely smiled, and gave Teacup a pat on the shoulder. "Don't worry, son. Nothing we can't handle."

5

Three hours of solid drinking. Damian was talking way too loudly, swearing so the whole pub could hear, reminiscing about stories no person in that place had any business knowing about. Dangerous stories about dangerous men, stories that could get people into trouble. The bartender was watching them closely. Teacup read the signs. It was time to go. He had it planned out in his head – first, another fag break, and then when the three were outside, a subtle suggestion that the place was way too boring, that they should move on. He couldn't imagine Damian disagreeing. He was wired. Itching to get to pastures new. Situation successfully diffused, for the present. And then a good while in the car, driving about, debating where to go, and then when they eventually reached their next destination, the whole thing would undoubtedly start again. But the way Teacup saw it, a new start was better than a bad finish.

And in the past few days, Teacup had seen lots of bad finishes.

Such was the plan.

They went out into the freezing cold air, and all three lit up.

There were four other people standing outside, two middle-aged couples, talking amongst themselves, laughing, each face illuminated by an orange dot of burning nicotine.

"Look at this crazy fucker!" Damian shouted suddenly. Everyone looked in the direction he was pointing. Up the hill, coming towards them, was a jogger. No, thought Teacup, as he focused on the individual about forty yards from them. This guy was running at speed, more than just jogging. And to run at that speed, in this chill and up such an incline, meant the guy was fit. Super fit. Teacup felt a trace of envy, and a little admiration. He could have done that five years earlier, when he was boxing. Not now though.

The runner dodged onto the road, to avoid them. Damian shouted some expletive. Thankfully the runner continued, hardly glancing at them.

"Why would people do that?" asked Damian, to no one in particular. "I mean seriously. Is he retarded or something? And in this fucking weather. His balls must be the size of peanuts. And his cock must be shrunk to the size of a .... what size does a cock shrink to, in this shitty bloody weather?"

Blakely took a deep drag of his cigarette. "A chipolata. Which is the equivalent to a miniature sausage."

"Yes, William," said Damian. "We all know what a fucking chipolata is. That's not the issue. The issue is... what in Christ's name is he doing, running like that in this weather? Doesn't make sense." He tapped his finger against the side of his head. "The guy's a moron."

Teacup tucked his hands in his coat pockets, against the cold. "Maybe. But he's a fit fucker."

The conversation drifted, and a silence fell. Teacup looked up, and in the sky was the blood moon. He gazed at it, entranced. It seemed perfect to him. A red circle, unblemished by cloud. Untainted. He had never seen anything quite like it.

Maybe an omen, he thought. A sign. Whether good or bad, he did not know. Usually bad, in his world. The four other people finished off their cigarettes, stubbed them out in an outdoor ashtray, and made their way in. A stillness fell. Beyond the periphery of the street lamp were shadows and darkness, and not much else. The world was holding its breath.

Teacup was not the type of man to soul-search. In his particular trade, it never paid to think too much about actions, consequences. Thinking could eat you up, consume you. Render a person ineffective. Yet now, at this moment, under this strange alien sky, he felt... what? A weight pressed in his mind.

Sadness.

He was here, in the village of Eaglesham, babysitting a psychopath. Along with a man who killed for money. The partygoers around him, smoking, drinking, laughing, were just people. Men and women, living normal lives, doing normal things. Two different worlds. His and theirs.

Teacup gazed up at the blood moon, looking for an answer. What was he, then? He was far from ordinary. He lived a life steeped in violence. Death. He had worked for Damian's father since he was in his teens. He was family, after all. It was a natural progression. A progression toward drug dealing, extortion, prostitution, racketeering. Murder. Every fucking sin imaginable, he thought grimly.

Far from ordinary. A gangster. Nothing more, nothing less. If he didn't end up in prison, he'd end up dead. Such were the career prospects, working for the Grants. He watched Damian from the corner of his eye. The guy was an emaciated drug-addicted fuck bag. But he was family. And he was Peter Grant's only child. And Teacup had a job to fulfil.

The sadness drifted away. The night lost its strange melancholy. An old emotion seeped into his heart. Bitterness. He was wasting his life. He raged against it. But there was nothing he could do. There was no way out. This was his job, pure and simple. And if you didn't like it, then in Peter Grant's world, you ended up in the ground, with a bullet in the head or a knife through the neck.

Teacup took a deep breath. *Christ, it's freezing,* he thought. It was time. He turned to Blakely. He opened his mouth, to suggest they move on, find another drinking hole, when Damian again pointed, arm stretched out, jumping up and down like an excited lapdog.

"Here he comes again, mad fucker! Can you believe this guy!"

Teacup and William Blakely, for the second time, jerked their heads round. Sure enough, the same runner was coming up the hill. If anything, noted Teacup, his pace had increased.

Damian turned to him, and spoke in a low whisper, in a tone which Teacup had learned to dread.

"So you think he's a fit fucker? Think a stab in the gut might slow him down?"

Damian produced a six-inch blade from inside his leather jacket.

Teacup did not reply. His heart rose to his mouth. He couldn't speak. The runner was only ten yards away and would be adjacent to them in two seconds. Damian suddenly dashed out towards him.

And then all hell broke loose.

6

Black approached the pub. He felt good. Relaxed. The limbs worked. The breathing was easy. The group outside had diminished, and he saw only three people. He increased his pace slightly, aware the smoker who had shouted at him might still be there. Get by them quick, he thought. He'd be past them in five seconds. He gave them a closer inspection as he neared. Three men. Well dressed. Two of them powerfully built, wide shoulders, bull necks, standing with the unmistakable poise of athletes. Trained men. Men who worked at their physiques. The third was slighter, with a pale, almost gaunt face, who suddenly pointed at him. Black felt a burst of renewed adrenaline, sensing trouble, and veered towards the far side of the road.

He was almost level. The man who had pointed, the smallest one, made a sudden move, sprinting out onto the road, directly into Black's path. Something flashed in his hand. A blade! The two others, like pack animals, came close behind.

Black could not avoid the situation. The events which followed were swift and devastating.

The man with the knife – Gaunt Face – lunged at him, trying to stab him in the midriff. The action was wild, uncontrolled.

Black stopped suddenly, twisted round, grabbed the man's arm in a lock, one hand on his wrist, the other just above the elbow, and thrust forward, snapping the ulna. The man's arm broke with an audible crack. He shrieked. Black shoved him away. The two others were on him instantly.

One swung a punch, hand glittering in the street light. A knuckleduster! Black ducked, took a step back. The other also threw a punch, a straight left, disciplined, accurate, like a boxer, trying to catch him as he ducked. Black raised his shoulder, absorbing the blow, but it felt like a slab had hit him.

Then Black did something they did not expect.

He attacked.

Knuckleduster took another swipe. Black stepped in, blocked the blow, kneed him in the groin, struck him a hard jab on the throat with the heel of his hand, crushing his windpipe. Knuckleduster gagged, staggered back. The Boxer jumped on his back, one arm in a strangle hold around his neck, inflicting short hard punches to the side of his face. Black butted him once, twice with the back of his head. The grip loosened. Both fell onto the road, the Boxer trying to swing Black under. Black relaxed, used the man's momentum, landed on top, struck his chin, his nose, heard the bones crunch. The Boxer produced a knife. Black disentangled, and with almost an acrobat's agility, spun away, and assumed a fighting crouch. Knuckleduster reappeared, lurched forward, but was in obvious distress, waving a six-inch blade. He swept his arm, trying to catch Black's throat. Black met him, caught his wrist, pulled him in, and brought a terrific blow to the man's temple. He toppled to the ground and lay still.

A manic scream cut the air. Gaunt Face, one arm flapping like a tube of rubber, slashed wildly at him, but with little focus. Black dodged, saw an opening, kicked his knee, which folded backwards. Gaunt Face howled, face contorted. Black hacked at his neck. Gaunt Face collapsed to the ground. Black crouched, dealt him a final blow, hard to the throat. He felt something snap. Gaunt Face rolled on his side, choking, body convulsing.

Black turned. The Boxer was still dazed, propped on one elbow, trying to get to his feet. Black loomed over him, stamped on his chest, his face. He heard the jaw break. The Boxer groaned. Black stamped again, then again, until the groaning stopped.

In less than thirty seconds, he had neutralised three armed men.

Black took a step back, tempted for a millisecond to melt into the darkness of the park. But the temptation passed. A young woman emerged from the pub, and saw him in the middle of the road, standing beside three men lying on the ground, and reacted as any normal human being would react.

She screamed.

"Call the police!" shouted Black. "Now!"

7

Don't stop to think; you attempt to rationalise and you'll die. You do exactly what you're trained to do. Thinking kills.

Staff Sergeant's message to new recruits of the 22nd Special Air Service Regiment.

The interview room was bare of any furniture, except a table and four chairs. No windows, the walls pale yellow, the colour of old puke, the floor dark-grey linoleum. The room was ferociously bright from a single strip light on the ceiling. On one side of the table against the wall was a tape-recording device, and a microphone. The only other item on the table was an empty plastic coffee cup.

Black was sitting on one of the chairs, and had been for twenty minutes, a uniformed policeman standing at the door.

Neither of them spoke. Black was in no mood for idle conversation. He had been given a brown sweat top and loose brown jogging trousers, which he was wearing. He was allowed to keep his socks. His original running gear had been photographed, samples had been taken by forensic analysts with surgical gloves, and then the clothing was bagged and taken away. He could still smell his own sweat. They had allowed him to wash off the blood from his face. Blood, he recalled, from men who'd attacked him less than two hours ago.

The door opened. Two men entered, non-uniform. One was bald and twenty-five pounds too heavy; small pinched features in a round bland face. The other was taller, wearing black-rimmed spectacles, hair growing an inch from his scalp like a dark bristle, a file tucked under his arm. Could have passed for an accountant instead of a police officer, Black thought. The uniformed policeman nodded and left, closing the door behind him.

The two sat opposite. The one with glasses placed the folder on the table, opened it to reveal a pad of white paper with handwritten notes. He took a pen from a pocket of his jacket, and started clicking the top.

"Just a few questions, Mr Black," he said. "A few details need clarification. You've phoned your solicitor, I understand?"

"Was there a need? But yes, I have. Shouldn't he be here before you start with your *few questions*? Legal representation, and all that. Not that I need one."

The policeman with the glasses did all the talking. He gave Black a thin-lipped smile, Black didn't detect a great deal of friendliness in it.

"Of course not. My name is DI Patterson, and this is DS Lomond. Just a few loose ends to tie up. We're asking for a little cooperation, Mr Black. That's all."

Black nodded.

"Your full name is Adam Black. And I believe you're a lawyer?"

Black nodded again. "Exactly what I told the duty sergeant. Exactly what's written in your notes."

"Okay. So, going through the series of events. You told the officer at the scene that you were out running?"

"Correct."

"Just running?"

Black looked levelly at the man wearing glasses.

"What's this about? I'm here cooperating. But I'm in an interview room without the recorder on, and without a lawyer, and you've taken my clothes. What do you mean, 'just running'? I don't get the question."

"There's nothing to get, Mr Black. We need to fill in some blanks."

"There are no blanks. There's nothing to fill in. It happened exactly as I said. It shouldn't be me here answering questions, but the bastards who attacked me."

There was a five second silence. And then DS Lomond cleared his throat.

"That won't be possible, Mr Black."

"Why is that?"

DS Lomond regarded him with a fixed stare.

Black waited.

"Two of the alleged attackers are dead." A pause. "Found dead at the scene. The other is in intensive care. For all I know he might be dead too. And the only witness is you, covered in blood. And not your own, as far as we can gather."

Black digested this information. He hadn't realised he'd killed them. Too bad.

The other one, DI Patterson, resumed his thin-lipped smile. As welcoming as a fucking alligator, thought Black.

"So, we have to be thorough, you understand. Every avenue needs to be pursued. You're a lawyer. You'll understand the need for us to explore this.... *situation,* as far as we can. You were running. You weren't out to meet anyone?"

"Nope."

"And you weren't carrying any weapons?" chimed DS Lomond. Unlike DI Patterson, he was not smiling. His face was expressionless, deadpan. Inscrutable.

"Of course not. When I run in the evening, I'm not inclined to get tooled up."

"You run a lot?"

"I do. You should try it."

Black thought he detected a flicker of annoyance on the face of DS Lomond. He was human, after all.

"And one of the individuals attacked you, unprovoked?" continued DI Patterson, ignoring the remark, studying the notes before him. "This is what you're saying."

"What I'm saying? Exactly right," replied Black. "With a knife. Followed by his two pals, who were also carrying knives. And a knuckleduster, if memory serves me correctly. That's right. You didn't mishear. A knuckleduster. And the funny thing about memory is this. When you're facing death, and it's close up, real close, right in your face, then everything suddenly appears in sharp relief, and the memory's usually pretty good about the detail. Wasn't there CCTV?"

"And you didn't know these men? This was a completely random attack?"

"Correct, and correct. Shouldn't you be writing all this down?"

"These men attacked you, for no good reason, and what happened then?"

"I defended myself."

Another silence fell. Both officers stared intently at Black, who stared right back.

"Have you any connection with the Grant family?" asked DS Lomond, suddenly. In the bright luminescence of the strip light, Black noticed he was not actually bald, but balding, with fine, almost invisible blond hair.

Black held his stare for three seconds.

"I'm not following the train of conversation. Who the hell are the Grant family?"

"What about the name Damian Grant? Or Tommy 'Teacup' Thomson?"

"Teacup who?"

DI Patterson scratched the back of his ear with his pen. He pursed his lips, as if measuring his next words, then spoke.

"There are some things which don't add up, Mr Black."

"Like what?"

Patterson frowned.

"Point number one – why on earth would three men, all apparently armed, suddenly attack a stranger in the street outside a busy pub, in a quiet village like Eaglesham. It doesn't make sen–"

"Unless they had a score to settle?" interrupted DS Lomond. "Maybe bad blood?"

Black shook his head. "Point number one is duly noted. But there's no point at all. You have this completely wrong. I had never met these men before. There's no bad blood. There's nothing. Sometimes the simplest theory really is the most plausible."

"Which is?" asked DI Patterson.

"That I was attacked for no reason by three psychopaths."

"But then there's point number two," said DS Lomond. "Which is what I'm trying to get my head round."

Black waited, but he had a good idea what point number two was all about.

"How can one unarmed man do so much damage to three armed attackers, and not have a scratch on him? That's what we don't understand."

8

─────────

Suddenly the door opened, and all three looked over.

A man entered, carrying a briefcase. He was dressed in jeans, polo-necked pullover, green waxed Barbour jacket, leather ankle boots; sharp, calculating eyes set in a tanned oval face; sandy buff hair. He was about forty, lean, and looked fit. He nodded at Black, who nodded back. He walked up to the table and appraised the two detectives.

"Gentlemen, my name is Simon Fletcher. I am Mr Black's appointed solicitor."

He didn't sit. Instead, he put his briefcase on the table.

"I'm hoping this briefcase doesn't need to be opened. Is my client under arrest?"

"Mr Black was very kindly helping us with our enquiries," answered DI Patterson. "No one's under arrest."

"I see. If he's only helping you with your enquiries, I'll take it that you will not be charging my client?"

"We need to keep an open mind. This is a serious incident, you understand. I might remind you, we can keep Mr Black for up to twenty-four hours."

Fletcher cleared his throat, as if he were about to begin a presentation.

"What I do understand is that Mr Black was attacked by three men, while out jogging. Yes?"

"That would appear to be the case, on the face of it."

"On the face of it. Which usually means that that's exactly what happened. Therefore, gentlemen, I'll repeat my question – you're not intending to charge my client?"

DI Patterson shook his head.

"If you're not intending to charge my client, there's seems to be no reasonable argument for detaining him any longer. Do we agree on this point?"

DI Patterson did not respond. DS Lomond's face remained impassive.

"But you've taken Mr Black's clothes, as if he's been treated like a suspect. Which I assume he's not. Did you take his shoes?"

"It's routine. You know that. We need to gather the evidence, sometimes as a formality. And yes, we took his shoes."

"Then it looks like I will need to open my briefcase," said Fletcher.

He clicked open two silver-coloured combination locks, opened it up, and produced a pair of training shoes, which he tossed to Black.

"Let's go, Adam. You don't need to be here anymore."

9

They made their way to an annex of the station, to a waiting room for members of the public, where Jennifer and their four-year-old daughter Merryn were waiting. The policeman escorting them nodded and left them at the entrance – two solid double doors.

"I can't go in just yet," said Black, leaning against the wall. He took a deep breath, and closed his eyes in an effort to calm his nerves. In the space of just over two hours, his world had taken a dramatic change. Life, suddenly, had a tinge of the surreal.

"What the hell happened out there?" asked Fletcher, in a voice low, urgent.

"Exactly what I said. Three guys, from nowhere. Fucking crazies. With knives. Plus, one had a knuckleduster, if you can believe it."

"Jesus," said Fletcher. "I'd no idea Eaglesham was such a war zone. So much for sedate country living. You'd better tell me everything. In the morning. Only if you're up to it, of course. Can't blame you if you need to take some time off."

"I'm fine. Just a little shaken. Nothing that a brandy can't fix. Or ten."

Fletcher gave a short humourless laugh. "It's been over fifteen years since I've walked into a police station. No idea if what I said was bullshit. Criminal law was never my *pièce de resistancé*. But I think my performance was... passable. Especially the briefcase bit."

"More than passable." Black grinned. "Bloody marvellous. You belong in the theatre. And thank you for the shoes. Though a bit tight."

Fletcher sniffed. "Beggars can't be choosers. Plus, I want them back."

"Of course you do." Black frowned. "It was strange."

"What?"

"I haven't been charged. They could have kept me in longer. It was almost as if they didn't know what to do. Like they were waiting. They questioned me without the conversation being taped. Asking me questions without legal representation. They weren't taking notes. Isn't that a little odd?"

"You're asking me? Give me a commercial contract before a police interview any day."

Black gave a weary smile. "It's been a long night. Thanks for coming. I didn't know who else to call. You're a good friend."

"You were attacked by three guys, and the cops have it all the wrong way around. It was the least I could do. You owe me big style, naturally."

"Naturally. I expect nothing less. Another thing. Just a minor detail. Two of the attackers died."

Fletcher's smile withered before him. His voice lowered to a rasping whisper. "Fucking one hell of a minor detail! Two guys dead?"

"And the police mentioned the Grant family. You heard of them?"

Fletcher visibly paled. He ran a fretful hand through his hair, his eyes blinking, as he computed the information.

"And you haven't? Where have you been? The fucking moon? Their reputation is one of blood and carnage. Not the type who turn the other cheek, if the stories are true. Which they are. Heavy fucking gangsters. Without alarming you, but they're mean bastards. To be avoided. Which is what you've not managed to do."

"I'm now duly alarmed."

"So you should be."

Black took a deep breath. It was his turn to swear. "Fuck."

10

When Black entered the waiting room, he saw that the only people occupying it were Jennifer and Merryn. It was a depressing place, the furniture comprising a row of blue plastic chairs along one wall and a low squat table with scattered out-of-date *Interior Design* magazines. A coffee machine was in a corner with a sign stating it was out of order. The lighting was the same strip lighting in the interview room. Bright, glaring. There were no windows, and the place was cold. *Rooms with no windows,* thought Black – *the architect should be shot.*

Merryn was in a pink and orange onesie, and lying across two seats under a blanket, asleep.

Jennifer rose to her feet.

"My God, Adam. What the hell's going on? I got a call from Simon..."

Black held her close, smelled the clean soap on her skin, the fragrance of her hair. She didn't belong in a place like this.

"I'll tell you back at the house," he whispered in her ear. "Over a drink."

Jennifer held him tighter. "What happened, Adam?"

"Shit happened. Unbelievable shit. But it's okay. It's all okay." He held her back a little and attempted a smile. "I guess it's soggy pasta."

She began to sob, and he held her again, thinking of the blood moon and her prediction of bad luck, and let the moment drift.

11

Damian Grant was dead. On the day of his funeral, two weeks after Christmas, the snow had stayed away, and the sun was bright on a chill morning. His father, Peter Grant, was not thinking about the weather on the day he buried his only son. His thoughts and heart were consumed with grief, as any parent would feel, committing their child to the earth. He lowered the coffin with five other bearers, all family or associates closely connected to the inner workings of the business. But he refused to shed any tears. Not his way. Tears were for weaklings, and Peter Grant was not weak.

The priest uttered a final prayer. Grant never heard a word. He tossed in a handful of dirt. The mourners dispersed, shaking his hand, hugging him, offering muted condolences. The reception was to be back at his house, where food and drink were laid in abundance, for Peter Grant had no intention of stinting on this day, the day of his son's funeral. But no alcohol would pass his lips. He was teetotal. He considered the act of getting drunk as weak and wasteful, almost sinful.

Thor waited at the door of the black Mercedes – Grant's

bodyguard, loosely described as his assistant. Six-foot-seven bodybuilder, his dark suit tight and pinched over his bulk. Hard, flat features, blond hair swept back and tied in a ponytail. A purple tattoo of a wolf's head emblazoned past his collar, halfway up his neck. From Berlin, he could barely speak a word of English. But he could break a man's neck like a dry twig. Grant got in, sat in the back seat, followed by Thor. The driver was his nephew, who eased the car off at a respectfully slow speed, along a single stony lane, chips crunching under the tyres, and out the cemetery.

"Is he here?" Peter Grant was sixty-five and looked ten years younger. He took care of his body. He had converted an annex of his Glasgow mansion into an ultra-modern state-of-the-art gym, and trained religiously early every morning before breakfast for an hour. He ran four miles every afternoon, cycled at the weekends. Twice a week he trained at a boxing club he owned in the east end of Glasgow. He neither drank nor smoked. He did not indulge in salt, sugar or red meat. Tanned, silver-haired, and flat-stomached, females found him attractive, but since the death of his wife ten years back, he took little interest in women. Rumour had it, his preference was handsome young men.

His nephew nodded – Nathan Grant: a quiet, unassuming man, intelligent and soft spoken, dark-haired, solemn features. Economics graduate from St Andrews University. First class honours. Best in his year. A young man who tried to avoid the physical side of the business, preferring books to violence. A serious young man, and a potential successor to the Peter Grant empire since Damian Grant's premature demise.

"He's just arrived. He's been shown to the conservatory."

"Fine. Give him what he wants. He likes cigars. Give him our best. And whisky. He likes that too."

Nathan Grant spoke into the handsfree on the dashboard,

another voice responded, acknowledging the instruction. Nothing more was said, as they drove back to Grant's mansion set in the leafy suburb of Whitecraigs, seven miles from Glasgow City centre.

12

The front gates were electric and opened as the car approached. Peter Grant's house was set back a hundred yards, behind manicured lawns shimmering with frost, and circular flower beds, devoid of flowers in the sub-zero temperature. The house was a listed building, formerly a Victorian nursing home, built of soft red sandstone with high arched windows and a high-peaked slate-grey roof. The frontage was the only vestige of the original building, a requirement under the planning laws. Peter Grant had flattened everything behind it, creating a brand-new structure, with ten bedrooms, squash court, gym, indoor pool, sauna, seven public rooms.

The car stopped at the entrance, and the three got out. They were met by a man dressed immaculately in dark suit and black tie. Other cars were following behind – mourners arriving for food and drink, and to say a final farewell to Damian Grant.

"He's in the conservatory, Mr Grant," said the man.

Grant glanced at Thor and Nathan beside him. "You two come with me."

They made their way through a wide, high hallway of sheer white marble walls, doors leading off on either side, to the rear quarters of the mansion, to the conservatory. This was Grant's sanctuary, where he sat, often alone, to reflect and plot. The outlook relaxed him, offered him a modicum of tranquillity, eased his mind – lawns pale green and flat as the baize of a pool table, stretched to a line of distant massive oak trees. In the centre he had created a pond with a little tinkling fountain, and arching across it was a Japanese moon bridge, with red and yellow wooden panels. At night, it was lit up with silken candle shades, and could have been a picture out of a fairy story. A million miles from the real world of Peter Grant, where there were no fairy tales, but drugs, prostitution, money laundering, extortion, death.

Sitting on a couch admiring this view, with a glass of whisky in one hand and a cigar in the other, was a bald, fat man in an open-collared shirt, V-neck sweater, cream flannels, suede hush puppies. He could have come straight from the golf course. He was markedly not dressed for a funeral. His head rested on a layer of chins, as he contemplated Peter Grant's back garden. He did not get up when the three men entered.

"Hello Mathew." Grant sat on a bamboo chaise lounge opposite. Between them was a low kidney-shaped mahogany table, and on it an ashtray and a manila folder.

Nathan stood behind him.

Thor remained at the door. "Hello Peter. A sad day. Sorry for not coming to the funeral. My presence there would have been a little... inappropriate?"

"Inappropriate," repeated Grant. "Now there's an understatement. I think for the chief constable to attend young Damian's funeral would be downright fucking *scandalous*. It wouldn't do that fat pension of yours any good. The tabloids would have a field day."

"True words," replied Chief Constable Mathew Smith. "But still a sad day." He shook his head dolefully, the droopy jowls of his face reverberating like a slobbery dog. "Such a tragedy. Cut off in his prime. A father should never have to bury his son."

Grant's face did not display an iota of emotion when he replied. "My son was a fucking halfwit scum-junkie, so we can cut the bullshit. Some would say he had it coming. Christ, I would probably have ended up killing him myself." Grant leaned forward. "But at the end of the day, he was my son. And I loved him. He was blood. My blood. And blood, being thicker than water and all that, must have its reckoning. Don't you think so, Mathew? You wouldn't like to see one of your own fall without a reckoning."

Smith took a sip of his whisky, and shifted uncomfortably on the couch.

"You have two sons, don't you, Mathew?" continued Grant. "You wouldn't like one of them to die in the street like a fucking dog."

"Bad business," said Smith.

"Fucking shit business!" shouted Grant suddenly, thumping his fist on the table. Smith darted his eyes, from Grant to his nephew standing behind him, to the looming presence of Thor. Mathew Smith was the highest-ranking policeman in the force, but that didn't stop him being nervous in the company of a man like Grant, who had a notoriously vicious temper which, when unleashed and unchecked, could end up bad for people.

Grant took a deep breath, straightening his back. Nathan, who knew his uncle better than most, produced a handkerchief from his top pocket and handed it to him. Grant took it, wiped his brow, and the flecks of saliva at the corners of his mouth.

"But you're right," said Grant eventually, his voice level. "Bad business. Because this is what it is, you understand. Business. Everything's business. There's nothing else. And in any business, things have to run smoothly. The wheels of industry have to keep turning. I can't allow any glitches in the profit-making process. When someone attacks my family, then they attack me – or more specifically, they attack my good name. And if it happens once, it can happen again, and again, until my name, and therefore my business, is flushed down the shitter. I can't allow this to happen. Life, like business, needs redress. The balance sheet has to... well, balance. So, old friend, tell me all about the cunt who killed my son."

Smith put his whisky glass on the table, and the cigar in the ashtray, and picked up the manila folder.

"It's all here. And it was not easy to get. Strings had to be pulled. Favours called in." Smith licked his lips. "Those wheels of industry need oil to turn. And the price of oil goes up, in certain situations."

"I can't disagree with that," said Grant. "You can't pay enough for good information." He turned his head to the side, and without looking at Nathan, said, "There's an envelope in the bureau. Get it."

Nathan left. Grant turned his attention back to Smith.

"Give me the gist."

Smith opened the file, which contained a sheaf of papers treasury-tagged together.

"This man is no Joe Ordinary. He is, how can I put it... unique."

13

Grant sat, still as a lizard in the sun, and listened.

"His name is Adam Black. He's forty-five. He was born in Hamilton. Both parents are dead. He had an older brother, who died during active service for the Royal Marines. If you go back five years, you'll not find anything exceptional. He's a partner with a law firm in town. Wilson, Fletcher and Co. Big in corporate stuff, apparently. A low-key high-fee firm with some nice clients. Discreet and dependable. For big hitters, they're a small outfit. Only three partners. Your average commercial firm in Glasgow has twenty. Black has been with the firm five years, was assumed a partner two years ago. His special fields are commercial conveyancing, contracts, company mergers. All in all, unspectacular. The only surprising thing is that he was made partner after a relatively short period of time. Which tells us something – either he's competent at his job, or he has friends in the firm."

"Or maybe both," suggested Grant.

"Maybe."

Smith turned some pages over. "But it's what he got up to

before then which creates a stir." He darted a glance at Grant, who remained immoveable, his face carved from granite.

"Adam Black graduated with honours from the University of Edinburgh, and then, at the age of twenty-one, decided on an unexpected career. Maybe something to do with his brother. He joined the army. He went to officer training at Sandhurst. Graduated top of his class, and at twenty-three, earned his maroon beret with the Parachute Regiment. He was Lieutenant in Second Battalion, where he spent two years, and thereafter volunteered for First Battalion which acts as a special forces support group. He was at this stage, twenty-six and was promoted to Captain.

"In 1995, Captain Adam Black was part of a peacekeeping corp seconded to a Special Services Group with the Pakistani Army. It was during this period when he had his first real taste of counterterrorist operations. Afghan hijackers had taken over a school bus, containing thirty primary school children and three teachers, and had driven to the Afghanistan Embassy in Islamabad, threatening to execute their captives unless demands were met. Captain Black, along with a contingent of three men from First Battalion, and the Pakistani Special Forces, stormed the embassy. The hijackers were killed, the hostages freed. The mission was a success. Black was regarded as something of a hero."

Nathan entered the room and handed Grant an A4-sized envelope. "More people are arriving," he said. "They've been taken to the dining room."

Grant nodded. "I'll be along shortly. Stay here. This makes for interesting listening."

Smith cast a hungry glance at the envelope on Grant's lap and continued.

"Captain Black was accepted into the 22nd SAS Regiment in

1997." He looked up again at his listening audience. "You can see why obtaining this information was so difficult. In 1998 he became part of a unit known as The Special Projects Team, a small internal group of the SAS concentrating on anti-hijacking and counterterrorism. Here, his dossier becomes understandably a little vague. What is certain is that he was second in command in Operation Barras, in 2000. A large gang of bandits known as the West Side Boys had kidnapped a group of British citizens in Sierra Leone, in difficult country known as the Occra Hills. The operation was nicknamed Operation Certain Death. He and his unit aided by fifty SAS Regulars parachuted in and rescued the hostages. A bloody little battle. Of the two hundred West Side Boys, an estimated one hundred and eighty were killed, buried in secret in the jungle. Information the government didn't want to share with the media. The SAS took no casualties. Again, further success for Adam Black. By this time, he had garnered quite a reputation."

Smith turned another page. Not a sound in the room, the silence heavy with portent.

"After that, oblique references are made to covert operations in Mogadishu and Bosnia, probably aiding in the hunt for war criminals. Also, two tours in Afghanistan.'

"And then we have Iraq, 2003. Black was part of Task Force Kill, involving deep covert excursions into the heartland of enemy territory. According to my sources, he carried out thirty combat missions. The last one, he was betrayed by an informant in an operation to assassinate General al–Maliki, Saddam Hussein's chemical expert. It was believed he was formulating anthrax. Black was captured with two of his men, and held in Saddam's infamous *basement* for forty days, until he escaped."

Smith looked up from the notes. He gave Grant a steady stare as he spoke.

"Black was awarded the Military Cross in 2004, and resigned

his commission in 2005. Upon his return to civilian life, he joined the law firm of Wilson, Fletcher and Co."

Smith closed the file.

"He married five years ago to Jennifer Walker. She's a doctor with Glasgow Royal. A paediatric consultant. She was head of her department, until four years ago, when she went part-time. They have a four-year-old daughter called Merryn. Details are all here." He tapped the file with his index finger. "You wouldn't believe the strings pulled to get all this."

Grant took a deep breath, absorbing the information, thoughts churning.

"Thank you, Mathew. Extremely thorough, as ever. There's an extra twenty thousand there, to repair all those pulled strings." He handed him the envelope, which Smith placed in a leather attaché case at his feet.

He stood, as did Grant, and they shook hands.

"This man is dangerous," said Smith. "Be careful what you start here."

Grant allowed the merest ghost of a smile to bend his lips. "He started it. My world is full of dangerous men. A world I've chosen. But he has his Achilles' heel. Blood is demanded, and blood will be given. Make no mistake."

Smith shrugged. "I don't care what you do to him. Just keep me out of it."

"But that's exactly what I expect. For you and that big gang of yours to stay out of it."

Smith hesitated. "And your cousin? Tommy? I understand he was pretty bad when they got him to hospital."

"Broken nose, dislocated shoulder, punctured lung, broken ribs, fractured skull. Plus, he's in a coma. Compliments of Captain Adam fucking Black."

14

The funeral made news the next day. Two columns in the broadsheets, a full double page in the tabloids, with accompanying pictures of both Damian and his father, and other pictures of known associates of the Grant family. Phrases such as 'gangland killing' and 'suspected hit' were splashed throughout.

"Sensationalist shit," judged Simon Fletcher, throwing two newspapers in the waste bin by the door. "Fucking morons. That's all there is to it."

Black was sitting at his desk. Since the incident, except for the Christmas and New Year holidays, he had not missed a day. *Keep Moving.* Two unforgettable words branded into his mind. And so much truth in them. After any intense conflict, whether mental or physical, the mind could rebel, seeking sanctuary from the real world. The symptoms were legion: depression, paranoia, schizophrenia, to name a few. Then followed the alcohol abuse, drug abuse, self-harm, suicide. Post-traumatic stress disorder was real. Black had witnessed its manifestations in friends and brothers in arms. Special Forces trained its soldiers to minimise the impact of PTSD – *keep moving.* Keep occupied. Focus on things around you. Externalise. Black himself had never experienced such a condition. It wasn't something he was smug about. Special Forces hand-picked their men. And the SAS preferred men who had the ability to deal with bad situations. And Black simply had that ability, in abundance. In any event, Black had been through a whole lot worse.

He rubbed his eyes. Jennifer, through worry, had been unable to sleep. And when she couldn't sleep, neither could he.

It was 7am. Both he and his partner Simon Fletcher started early, and often finished late. The third and founding partner, John Wilson, was almost part-time, and about to retire at sixty-five. He strolled in, and strolled out, and had given up handling any real work weeks ago. His hobby was golf, and red wine. And young ladies, since his divorce. Both Black and Fletcher had agreed a replacement was unnecessary when he finally went. They'd take on the extra caseload and see their profit stake rise.

"Maybe," said Black. "We can't escape the inescapable – which is the fact that I killed the man's son."

"When he tried to kill you."

"It is what it is. What worries me is what will be. God, I'm tired."

"You look it. The three of you need to get the hell away from this shit. For a few days. Please, humour me. You need to chill. I can handle your stuff while you're gone. Fuck, I'll even wheel old Wilson in to lend a hand, if I can get him off the golf course. Or the club bar."

"Get away? Maybe. But to do what. Talk it through? There's nothing to talk about. Jennifer's worried about repercussions, and who can blame her. By sheer bad luck, we're on the radar of the mob. Getting away isn't going to cure that particular problem."

"Perhaps not. But it might relax the mind. Gain a sense of perspective."

Black gave a wintry grin. "From where I sit, the perspective is perfectly clear. Peter Grant has buried his son, who now lies cold in a coffin. And he's blaming me for it. I can go away and ponder the vagaries of life, or deal with the here and now, which is plough through a pile of work." He gestured to a column of files on his desk two feet high. "I have transactions coming out my ears. I would rather lose myself in these than lose my fucking mind."

"And Jennifer? What about her mind? She's sick with worry. You've just said she can't sleep."

Black gazed at the photo of his wife and daughter on his desk. Laughing on a warm day on a beach. Except for that, a notepad, the files, a phone and a computer screen with keypad, there was little else. Nothing unnecessary. Clear desk mentality, perhaps a legacy from army discipline. Simon Fletcher's desk on the other hand was so cluttered, you could stir it.

"You're right, of course. But at this moment, there's absolutely nothing I can do about that. I can't even say how different it would be if I could turn the clock back. Because it would be the same. Two guys dead and me still standing. The third guy was lucky."

"Lucky?"

"Lucky to be alive."

"Fair enough." Fletcher raised his hands in defeat. "Adam Black knows best. I guess I'm concerned about my old buddy. And his family."

"Don't be. Honestly. We'll get through this."

Fletcher stood. "They never taught us about any of this kind of shit at university."

"It's life. You learn by living it."

"Some fucking life."

Suddenly the phone rang, the call coming through directly after two minutes if the receptionists weren't picking up. Someone forgot to put the answering machine on. Their receptionists didn't arrive until 9am. Normally, by way of instinct, Black would have picked up, and answered himself. A distraught client; an important message; a lawyer needing to close a deal urgently. But since that night in Eaglesham, the phones had been incessant. For all the wrong reasons.

Black cast a quick look at Fletcher.

"Ignore it," said Fletcher.

"Fuck it. It might be important." Black picked up.

"Is that Adam Black?" spoke a male voice, sounding way too animated for that time in the morning.

"Who's asking?"

"Only two minutes of your time, Mr Black," continued the voice, rattling out the words, so quick Black had barely time to breath. "How well did you know Damian Grant? An old school friend? How did you meet? What's your connection with the Grant family?"

Black hung up.

"The papers?"

"Why the hell can't they stay away," said Black. "Vultures. They can smell a carcass a mile away."

"Is that what you are? A carcass?"

Black twitched his head, gave a wry smile. "Not yet."

"It's their job. It doesn't really matter what you say, or what you don't say, they'll make it up anyway, because they don't give a fuck. Ignore them and they'll go away. Like an itch in the balls. You just have to ride it out."

"Interesting comparison," Black mused. "I just hope it's that simple. Somehow I think this mess is here to stay."

The phone rang again.

"I'll take care of this." Fletcher stretched over and picked the phone up.

"Now listen..." He frowned and handed the phone to Black.

"It's Jennifer. She says she's been trying to call you on the mobile. She says there are two men outside your house."

15

Fear is just a state of mind. Meet it, feel it, bask in it. Make it your friend. Once you've done that, I kid you not, the world is yours to conquer.

Address to new recruits of the 22nd Special Air Service Regiment.

Their house was one of four cottages built on roughly two acres of land. The original buildings were old and solid, constructed about a hundred and twenty years earlier for tenant farmers. They had been enlarged and modernised over time, each standing on its own half acre, each separated from the other with mature trees and bushes and leafy borders. It was love at first sight, at least for Jennifer, with its white stucco walls laced with lush crimson ivy, its rust-red slated roof, its secluded garden. Quaint and private. Country but not quite country. Amenities only a mile away. They were about fifty yards from the main road, accessed by a single private lane, the lane running by the houses, two on each side, coming to a turning point at its dead end – a hammer-head.

To get to the house from his office would normally take Black, driving his Mini Cooper at sedate speed, about thirty-five minutes. When he got the call from Jennifer, he was there in twenty.

He saw it immediately when he pulled into the lane. At the top, fifty yards from their house and parked in the hammer-head, a shining, gunmetal grey 7 series BMW, with brand new licence plates.

He pulled up outside his own house. Jennifer was standing at the front door, Merryn beside her, holding hands, Merryn dressed for nursery, Jennifer for work.

Black got out, made his way up to them.

"It might be nothing," she said. She was pale, exhaustion etched on her face, her hazel-brown eyes heavy with lack of sleep. "I saw it drive up about a half hour ago. It's just sitting there. There's two men in it. No one's got out. No one's doing anything. I didn't know whether I should call the police. But then if I did, they'd probably think I was crazy. I probably am. I'm so sorry, Adam." Tears welled up; her mouth quivered, as she stifled a sob. "The whole thing is crazy."

"You're not crazy," soothed Black. He held her and spoke gently in her ear. "It's a mess right now. But it'll clear up. We need to give it time. They're probably more journalists, trying to get a scoop. Maybe this is the reaction they wanted. To try to get me to speak to them. Merryn's ready for nursery, so go to work, and act like everything's normal. Soon it will be normal. I promise."

He cupped her chin in his hands, looked into her eyes.

"I promise."

"You sure?"

Black nodded.

"What are you going to do?"

"Have a chat. As a concerned neighbour."

"Then we'll stay right here."

Black gave a small half-smile. "Fair enough. I won't be long."

16

The engine was running; Black ambled towards what was easily a seventy-thousand-pound-plus luxury car. Brand new, probably hours from the showroom. The two occupants inside did not look the type who belonged in such a vehicle.

They watched him as he approached, and Black watched them back, giving a friendly nod. The driver had a shaved head, skull-faced, bone-white complexion, drawn features, shadows under small darting eyes. A drug user, Black surmised. Not your typical journalist type. Probably no more than twenty-two, but looked much older. The passenger was altogether different. Flat face, solid chin showing a day's grizzle, a heavy beetling brow; short copper-coloured hair. Flat splayed nose. He wore a blue hoodie, but it couldn't disguise wide shoulders, a strong muscular build. He was older, maybe thirty, thought Black. Nor was he a journalist – perhaps a boxer. Or a wrestler. A man who exuded easy violence.

Black sauntered up to the driver's side, showing an affable smile, and tapped the window with the back of his hand. The driver looked up at him and smiled, revealing a row of brown, rotten teeth. The window slid down.

"Good morning, gentlemen," said Black, leaning forward slightly.

The driver spoke. "Cold morning." The passenger craned his neck, and met Black with an intense stare, but remained silent.

"And it's going to get a lot colder," replied Black. "So the weatherman predicts."

The driver nodded. "I hear that. A lot worse. Maybe snow."

"Maybe. But you guys won't be feeling too much of the cold with the engine running and the heater on. It'll be like a nice summer day in your beautiful new car."

"I'd rather be in here than out there, that's for sure," said the driver. "Big freeze coming." The passenger didn't take his eyes off Black.

"A strange place to be sitting in such a lovely car. And on such a cold morning. And so early. Thought you young men would be tucked up in bed at this time. Together." Black waited for a reaction.

The driver's smile faded, as he absorbed what Black had said. Suddenly he found his smile again. "We're admiring the view. Was that your wife I saw you talking to? You're a very lucky man."

Black nodded.

"And that would be your little girl. Merryn? Is that her name? She must be what, four?"

"You're good with names," said Black.

"I never forget a name or a face. It's a talent. A gift, you might call it. Me and my mate would love to meet your wife. And your daughter. Maybe not today. But someday soon. Very soon, I hope."

Black gave him a quizzical look. "Well, it can't be today for sure."

The man in the passenger seat suddenly spoke, his voice

harsh. "It can be any fucking day we want. And that's a message from Mr Grant. So shut the fuck up!"

"But it can't be today," responded Black in a quiet even tone. "You're too busy."

"What?"

"You've got two important appointments. First appointment is the garage."

Black was holding a set of keys, and using the tip of his house key, he scored a deep line down the driver's door. It made a dull grating sound. The driver swore, and tried to get out, but Black, standing close up, slammed the door shut with his knee.

The passenger got out. He was bigger than Black had first thought, maybe six-four, a clear two inches taller than Black. Black tensed, waiting for him to come round. Instead, he stayed on his side of the car, and glared at Black across the roof. Black guessed he wouldn't make a move. This was to be a message only. Grant was toying with him. A preliminary round, and Black wasn't to be touched. Not yet.

"You'll fucking pay for that!"

"Not me. But I reckon you will. Maybe a couple of grand for new paintwork. But if it's a whole new door…"

"Fuck you."

"Don't forget you've got a second appointment."

"What?"

"With the hospital."

Black had clenched his hand into a fist, the tip of the key protruding by an inch from between his curled fingers. The driver, window down, was staring up at him, all remnants of a smile vanished. Black struck him twice hard in the face, ensuring the point of the key penetrated his eye. The man screamed, as his eye popped in a small explosion of blood. Black gripped the back of the man's head and slammed his face against the steering wheel.

The man rebounded, dazed.

Black leaned in, grabbed the driver by the throat, his mouth an inch from his ear. "You mention my wife or daughter again..." he said in a low whisper, "...you even so much as think about them, and I'll blind you in the other eye, you fucking junkie fuck." Black slammed his face once again hard onto the steering wheel.

He straightened. The man opposite was wavering, unsure of his next move. Events had taken an unexpected twist. Black had met many men like him. A big muscular heavy sent to intimidate the intended victim, to terrify. To extort the vulnerable. But turn the tables, and they were revealed to be nothing more than show. Pretend hardmen. Glorified message-bearers.

"You'd better hurry, or your handsome friend is going to bleed all over your leather upholstery. And Mr Grant wouldn't want that."

"Next time I'll fucking rip your face off." The man ducked his head back into the car. "Swap over. I'll drive!"

Black took several steps back. The driver opened his door, lurched out, and staggered round to the passenger side, hands wrapped round his face, blood pouring at an alarming rate, the front of his pullover saturated.

The big man swapped places, moving round to the driver's side. He scowled at Black, but said nothing.

He got in. "There's fucking blood on the seat!" Black heard him say.

The car swept away, tyres screeching.

Black walked back the fifty yards to his house, where Jennifer and Merryn were still waiting at the front door.

"I heard shouting," she said. "Who were these men?"

"They were out to get a reaction. But I didn't say the things they wanted to hear, and I guess they got a tad annoyed."

"Newspapers. Next time they come around, I'm calling the police. This is harassment. This is where we live. It's an invasion of privacy!"

"If there is a next time." He took her hand. "If you see anything strange, or you're not sure about something, or something doesn't look right, then you call the police. And me."

"Then pick up your fucking mobile phone!" She hugged him. "You've got blood on your collar."

Black smiled. "I'll change. Must have cut myself shaving."

17

Over the years, Peter Grant had learned to keep a close rein on his emotions. It had proved to be a useful skill. Those close to him, and those not so close, never knew what he was thinking, and could not easily predict his next move, which was usually something unexpected. Since his son's death, Grant's mask of cool detachment would slip occasionally, sometimes for no apparent reason, and when it did, Grant displayed all the attributes of a vicious sociopath. Wild, uncontrolled. Savage. When he was told about the incident at Black's house, he didn't react as Nathan had anticipated.

Nathan had chosen to drive out to Grant, to tell him personally. If bad news were to be imparted, Grant preferred it to be given personally, man to man, and Nathan knew there was no other way to get around it. Damian had been buried only the day before, his body still warm in the grave. It was no wonder Nathan's stomach fluttered with dread.

Peter Grant owned a large portfolio of properties, not only in Glasgow, but throughout the length and breadth of Scotland, including Edinburgh. And most of his properties were in prime locations. One such location was a bijou wine bar on ultra-trendy Leith Walk, two miles from Edinburgh city centre overlooking the River Leith – The Pelican's Eye. Kitted out with rich cedarwood décor and handcrafted furnishings, solid yet graceful – the drinks were expensive, the food extortionate. But tourists liked the intimacy, paid the prices, and profits were up, which made Grant a happy man. In due course, he would sell, make a heap of money, and move on to the next project.

Grant was in The Pelican's Eye, enjoying a flat white coffee, ground from fresh excelsa beans, and when Nathan Grant met his uncle, after driving the fifty-mile journey from Glasgow, he was sitting outside the wine bar on a pedestrianised cobbled walkway at a little wooden table under a green awning, only ten yards from the river. It was plus-one degree Celsius, the morning bright and sharp. Peter Grant seemed oblivious to the cold, and as ever, when Nathan saw him, he was dressed immaculately – navy-blue, close-fitting suit woven from Italian wool, silk shirt, matching blue tie; calf leather brogues.

The picture of sophistication. Elegance.

He was sitting alone. On the table before him was a cup and saucer, and a mobile phone.

When Nathan sat beside him, he spied the unmistakable form of Thor, sitting inside, watching his master from the shadows, a sombre presence.

Before Nathan could utter a word, the mobile on the table vibrated.

Grant nodded at Nathan, raised a finger to his mouth, indicating silence.

He picked the phone up. It was impossible for Nathan to make out the other voice, but whoever it was did a lot of talking. Grant listened, staring at nothing. And then he spoke.

"It's going to be fine. Abacus is almost set up. Just a bit longer. Maybe eight or nine weeks. We're near the finishing line. There's no going back now."

The voice spoke for a while. Nathan was mildly surprised at Grant's patience. Whoever was speaking was important enough for Peter Grant to listen to.

"It's taken care of. The fly in the ointment is one fucking dead fly. I promise you. Abacus can push ahead. Relax."

The voice again.

"Stop whining. The problem will be resolved, and you can worry all you want while you're getting your dick stroked on some beach in the fucking Caribbean. I've got this covered. It will be dealt with. No problem."

The voice again, and then Grant hung up, and placed the phone back on the table.

"So, what happened? If there's a need for you to drive all the way out here to ruin my coffee, then I'm assuming that what you're about to tell me is not good. What's up?"

Nathan ran his fingers through his hair. This was his uncle he was talking to, his blood, but the fear of disappointing him was far greater than the fear of his anger. Though his anger was terrible to behold. He decided to approach it by an indirect route. "That sounded a serious conversation."

"Very."

"I don't think I've heard of Abacus. New venture?"

"Huge venture, more like. And you won't have heard of it, because it's what's defined as 'fucking confidential'. But you'll know soon enough. It'll keep you busy for a long time. So, I repeat – what the fuck is up?"

"There was a situation this morning."

Grant remained still. He had an ability to look uncannily calm, which Nathan found to be unnerving, if not bloody terrifying. Calm before the storm. And Grant was the living embodiment of a perfect storm. Nathan found he couldn't look his uncle in the eye.

"I got the boys to wait outside Black's house, exactly as you wanted. Early this morning. They made sure his wife saw them as she was going to work. To frighten her, give her a wake-up call. As you asked."

"And?"

"There was a situation."

"You've just said that. What the fuck is wrong with you?"

The veneer was slipping, thought Nathan. "She must have called Black. He came home, while the boys were there."

"What did you expect him to do? He's not the type to ignore a thing like that. And?"

"Black scored the side of the car. And he blinded Jimmy. Punctured his eyeball with a car key. The guy's a fucking maniac."

Grant took a sip of coffee, licked his lips, replaced the cup delicately on the saucer.

"And Black? My orders were that he was not to be touched."

"They drove off. Black wasn't touched."

Grant gave an almost imperceptible shake of his head. "So, what's the problem? I don't give a shit if Jimmy the scum-junkie loses his eye. He's got another one. And he got paid, didn't he? Risks of the job. Black could have torn his fucking limbs off, for all I cared. So long as he knew we were there. And now he knows he's not the one. Now he's got to look to his wife and kid." Grant took another sip of his coffee. When he spoke, his voice was low and soft. "He took my only child from me. He needs to know there's a price to be paid."

"Okay. So, we send the letters?"

Grant nodded. "In a couple of days. But we have to be patient. This is something we need to savour." He called over a waitress and ordered two fresh coffees. When she was out of earshot, he leaned over, beckoning Nathan closer.

"And not one hair on Black's head is to be touched. Not yet. He's got to know this was all his doing, you understand? He's got to know what this feels like. And then, when the deed is done, and he's lost everything, then I rip his fucking throat out."

He sat back. The edges of his mouth lifted into the semblance of a smile.

"We have to pay a visit today."

Nathan frowned. "Who?"

"Teacup. Haven't you heard?"

"What?"

"He's woken up."

18

"Tell me about him. This man. This *Adam Black*."

The extent of his injuries had rendered Teacup in a comatose state for just over three weeks, but it couldn't wait, apparently. Business as usual. He lay in a room in a private hospital in the south side of Glasgow, propped up on two pillows, every breath like broken glass scraping the innards of his chest. Several cracked ribs, a punctured lung, plus other wounds, courtesy of the man whose name had just been mentioned. But the individual at his bedside was not someone to be brushed away. Incapacity and injury had to wait in line. The individual was his relative and boss, Peter Grant, the man paying the hospital bills. The man who paid everything. The man who had lost his only son. On Teacup's watch. He tried to mask the fear from his voice. "It's vague. I can't remember much. And it was dark."

Grant sat on a plastic chair, taut posture, back straight as a lance. The air was suffused with the sweet, heavy scent of his cologne. Teacup felt nauseous. On the other side of the bed, sat Nathan. Quiet, studious-looking. Teacup had always liked him.

At the door, watchful and brooding, stood Grant's bodyguard, the man called Thor.

"It was dark," echoed Grant, gazing at Teacup. He turned to Nathan. "You're the one with the brains. So maybe you can correct me, but isn't it always dark at night-time. Or am I being stupid."

Nathan didn't reply.

Grant focused back on Teacup. "It was dark. Everything was vague." Grant leant forward, lowering his voice. "What type of answers are these, exactly? This is the night my son was killed in the street like an animal. Think back, Teacup. I'm sure you can do better."

Teacup swallowed, grimaced, the act causing pain. "We decided to have some drinks in Eaglesham. I thought, a quiet place. I thought..."

"You thought – a quiet place, no trouble. Where my psychopathic son wouldn't create a scene."

Teacup shook his head. The movement caused his mind to ache. "Nothing like that. We agreed a change would be... good for everybody."

Grant didn't respond. He stared at Teacup, eyes like black stones.

"We had some drinks," Teacup continued. "We were outside, having a fag. We saw this guy running up the hill, towards us."

"Running?" said Nathan.

Teacup nodded. "He was jogging. But going fast. Like he was trained."

Teacup revisited the scene in his mind. He had awakened from oblivion, and it was there, filling his brain. Every detail. He'd tried to shut it out, close the door, but it sat there, not shifting, a weight in his head.

"The truth is..." he faltered.

"The truth is?"

Teacup took a deep breath, which hurt. "Damian had a knife. He was going to use it. He saw the guy. He wanted to have a bit of fun. He ran out, onto the road. Probably just to scare him."

"Just to scare him," repeated Grant.

"The guy Adam Black is big. And he moved quickly for a big guy. And he wasn't scared. He reacted like he knew what he was doing."

"And you and Blakely? Where were you two when Black was killing my son."

"We were on him, I swear. At the same time. But..."

"But what?"

"He went through us, as if we weren't there."

"Three of you," said Nathan, in a quiet voice. "Against one man."

Grant's gaze didn't waver.

"He was fast," said Teacup. "And something else. I was on the ground. But he kept coming. Most men would have pulled back, maybe run away. But he kept coming, like..."

"Like what?" said Nathan.

"Like he enjoyed it."

A silence fell.

Eventually Grant spoke.

"So, you're telling me this was a random event. A guy comes running up the street, out of nowhere, a fight starts, my son ends up dead. A coincidence."

"That's all it was. We got into a fight. But with the wrong guy. Look at me. I'm lucky to be alive."

Grant stood, and regarded Teacup for five seconds. "Too fucking right."

Without a further word, he left the room, Nathan and Thor following.

Teacup relaxed on the pillows, wondering how this would end. Not good, he thought dismally. For everyone.

They left the hospital, and got into a white Mercedes, parked in the visitors area.

"What do you think?" Nathan asked.

"About what?" Grant snapped.

"Teacup's story."

Grant paused, then said, "I believe him. His injuries speak for themselves. Seems like Black likes to dish out a bit of pain. Which is fine by me. He's in my world now. He won't know the meaning of the word when I get him." He looked round to Nathan, sitting with him in the back seat, Thor driving.

"But one thing I don't buy."

Nathan waited.

"I don't believe in coincidences."

"I don't understand."

"You will, in time. It could mean everything, or nothing."

19

Three days had passed since the so-called 'situation' outside his house. Black had decided against contacting the police. He had stabbed a key in a man's eye and vandalised his car. It didn't look good. He thought it prudent to let that one pass. And he was secure in the knowledge that his victim would do the same.

But they knew where he lived. They knew he was married and had a four-year-old daughter. Christ, they knew her name. Grant had sent a message, and Black had sent one back. That he was not scared of them. That he could administer casual violence as easily as them. But Jennifer and Merryn were in the equation, and the stakes had never been higher. They could hide away, but for how long? And how could they live like that, scurrying through life like frightened animals? Looking over their shoulder, every minute, every second.

There was no easy solution. They had to continue their routine, go about their normal lives. Merryn was too young to understand what was going on. Jennifer was terrified. She didn't say, but Black knew she was, and who could blame her? And there was nothing he could do about it. For the first time in his life, he felt ineffectual. He had suggested she take an extended break from work – she was more than due it – and she and Merryn stay with her mother in her big house in Thurso, over one hundred miles north of Inverness, as about as far north as most people go. But he had only suggested it tentatively, and she had flatly refused, which was the best thing, reflected Black. Grant was clearly resourceful. He would find out where she'd gone. And if that happened, Black was nearly three hundred miles away to do anything about it.

Black restructured his hours, left the house in the morning when Jennifer and Merryn left, and got back early, taking files home. They stayed in during the evening and watched television, read books.

Life went on. For three days. Then it began.

The unravelling of Black's life.

20

Ten thirty in the morning, and Black was in the meeting room – the largest room in the offices of Wilson, Fletcher and Co., east-facing, pale morning sunlight captured by three large windows. One entire wall was dedicated to oak-panelled shelving for hundreds of law books, journals, reports, and in the centre a large rectangular walnut-veneered conference table with ten chairs round it, the surface gleaming. Black was sitting on one side, with three clients opposite, and between them were papers and plans and open files. The smell of fresh filtered coffee filled the room.

The door opened. Black turned. Rarely was anyone permitted to interrupt at a meeting, unless it was prearranged, or a secretary was bringing a file or a coffee.

Simon Fletcher stood at the doorway. He didn't speak. He didn't enter. He was ghastly pale. He looked shocked. His shirt collar was unbuttoned, his tie askew.

"What's up, Simon?" asked Black, holding down sudden panic. Something was way wrong, his first thoughts Jennifer and Merryn.

Fletcher licked his lips, took a stuttering breath, but didn't respond.

"Excuse me," said Black to the three people opposite, each reacting with looks of mild bemusement. He got up and made his way over to Fletcher who watched him approach with a glazed faraway stare.

Fletcher stepped back into the hallway; Black followed, closing the door behind him.

"What the hell's the matter, Simon?" asked Black, his voice low, strained.

"I got a call from John Wilson this morning," replied Fletcher, in a brittle voice. He kept swallowing, the muscles in his jaw clenching, unclenching. His eyes wouldn't fix on Black but darted left and right. *He's scared,* thought Black.

"John Wilson?" Black was trying to grasp the problem. The last name he was expecting to hear was that of his retiring partner. "And?"

"I didn't know what to do. I've never seen anything like it. I... don't know what to do."

Black had no option – he grabbed Fletcher by the shoulders and shook him.

"Speak to me, Simon!"

Fletcher seemed to wake out of a trance. He took a deep breath.

"John Wilson is dead."

21

Hurried excuses were made; the three clients in the meeting room were told an emergency had arisen; apologies were duly given; an appointment was rescheduled. Now it was Fletcher sitting in the meeting room opposite Black, and completely against office policy, smoking a Marlboro Red. Black didn't give a damn. He opened a window, and then sat, watching Fletcher inhale deep lungfuls of nicotine. Fletcher had found his voice and was now in talk overload. *Shock*, Black thought.

"I got a call from John, this morning," Fletcher said between drags. "He sounded... not like himself. Worried. You know John. The most laidback man in the world. You only caught him stressed if he missed a putt on the eighteenth. Couldn't keep him away from that damned golf course. He's got a son. In Australia, I think."

Another drag. Black waited. No point in hurrying this, though he had to grit his teeth.

"He was definitely not himself. He told me to come over. To his house. He didn't ask. He fucking *told*. Then he got angry. Like he was blaming the world for his problems. Started going on about his life, and how shit it was. I said 'John, you've got to calm the hell down'."

He gave Black a sudden hollow, stricken look. "If I had known what he was going to do..."

Another deep drag.

"So, I stopped everything. You know how difficult it is to do that in our job. I almost resented him for it. I *did* resent him for it. As if I've got the time to spare. I mean, he's the one that was retiring. But I did. I dropped everything, got in the car, and drove to his house. It felt like forever. Red lights every hundred yards. Would have been quicker walking. So, I got to his house, and walked up his front path, having to stop myself from tripping up on weeds and shit. He was never a gardener."

Another drag. Smoke coiled about him like shadowy grey tentacles. He stopped, eyes distant.

"And then what happened?" asked Black gently.

Fletcher focused again, took another smoke. His hand was trembling.

"The front door was open. Just a little. But I thought, *This is fucking odd.* Who keeps their front door open? And I knew right at that moment that something was bad." He shook his head. "I shouldn't have gone in. I shouldn't have entered his house. Why did I go in?"

Another pause.

"But you did go in," prompted Black.

"Yes. I did go in. He wasn't about. I was in his hallway. I shouted for him, but I didn't get an answer. So, I made my way through to that stupid television room he has. And the first thing I see is that sixty-inch projector television. It takes up a whole side of the room, I swear. Like a fucking cinema screen. Who needs something like that? And it's dark, because he's closed his blinds. And so, I turn around... I turn around."

Black waited.

"The silly bastard's hanging there. I mean fucking *hanging*. Face all twisted. A length of rope round his neck. His tongue was sticking out. His tongue was purple. Fucking purple! His eyes were bulging out their fucking sockets. I can't get it out my mind."

Black absorbed this information and kept his voice level.

"And what did you do, Simon?"

He stared fixedly at Black, stubbing out the butt of his cigarette on a saucer improvising as an ashtray; blinked.

"I ran the hell out of there and came straight here."

Black stared back, dumbfounded.

"You left him there? Simon, how do you know he was dead? Did you phone for an ambulance?"

"I know a dead man when I see one," he mumbled.

"Really? And did you phone for an ambulance?"

Fletcher shook his head, fumbling for another cigarette. Black stretched over and knocked them out of his hand. Fletcher snapped his head up.

"No time for smoking," said Black, perhaps a little too roughly. "We're going there now. We'll take your car. Right now."

22

Black insisted he would drive – he was in no mood for an argument. Fletcher was distracted, to put it mildly. Black had no desire to end up wrapped around a lamp post. The day was bad enough already.

Fletcher liked his cars. They got into a BMW Z4, convertible, with all the trimmings. Black stepped on the gas. He knew where to go. He had been to John Wilson's house on many occasions – for dinner, for meetings, for barbecues, for drinking sessions. He was a man who loved life. If he wasn't golfing, he was on holiday. He was divorced, but he had girlfriends. He was fit and healthy, as far as Black knew. He was planning to retire and talked about it almost every time the men spoke. He was planning to go to Australia to see his son. Lots of plans. Suicide didn't make sense. But then, who understood the dark paths the mind could wander.

Fletcher and Black didn't talk in the car, each consumed in their own thoughts. Fletcher lit up again. Black didn't object, but he opened his window. The cold winter morning sharpened his senses, cleared his mind.

Suicide didn't make sense.

They got to his house in fifteen minutes. John Wilson lived in an upmarket part of the west end; a mid-terraced Edwardian sandstone house in the middle of a row of similar houses, with mature trees growing on the pavement, and ivy walls, gleaming black balustrades and high gothic-style windows, with deceivingly large back gardens. Two hundred yards from the trendiest restaurants and wine bars in the city, two miles from the city centre. Premium location, premium price.

"I can't go in," said Fletcher. "I just can't. I'll wait in the car. Please."

Black acknowledged his plea with the merest nod, got out of the car, and ran to the house. There was no time to debate.

The door was closed but not locked. He pushed it open and entered a wide hallway, dark with oak panelling. For a single man, John Wilson kept a neat house. But then, he had always been fastidious, both in his work and in his life. He made his way directly to the television room. There along one wall, the monster television. It was semi-dark. As Fletcher had said, the blinds were closed. In the corner, he found John Wilson. And as Fletcher had recounted, he was hanging with a rope noose around his neck. He had used a dining room chair. It was toppled over at his feet. He had kicked it away. The rope was tied to a metal shelf bracket sticking out from the wall, secure enough to take the weight of a body.

Black repositioned the chair, stood on it, and hoisted John Wilson's limp body up with one arm. He was a small, slight man, no more than a hundred and forty-five pounds. But a limp body was still heavy. With his free hand, Black tugged loose the rope around his friend's neck. Fletcher had been accurate in his description. The face only an inch from Black's was ghastly to behold.

He loosened the rope enough to pull it over Wilson's head, which slumped against Black's shoulder. Carefully, he manoeuvred the body and himself onto ground level, and laid him out flat on the carpet. Black immediately performed CPR, placing the heel of his hand on his chest, placing the other hand on top, and started to press. No reaction. Black had seen death before, close up, and saw it now. But he had to keep trying. He performed a rescue breath, tilting Wilson's head, lifting his chin. Nothing. Once more, and then a third time.

Black collapsed onto the floor, and lay beside the still body of his friend and founding partner of Wilson, Fletcher and Co.

"Fuck!" Black shouted at the ceiling, at the world.

23

Black lay for less than a minute, mind racing, then got up.

Suicide didn't make sense. Not for a man like John Wilson. Black looked about. There was no obvious sign of a note, a sealed envelope, a farewell letter explaining the whys and the wherefores. Which meant nothing. There could be a note anywhere in the house, or there might be none at all. A sex game gone wrong? Possible, but not probable. And he had phoned Fletcher earlier in a black mood. An angry mood. To Black's mind, strange behaviour for a man poised to tie a rope round his neck. He examined the body. Marks on the backs of his hands – scuff marks. Wilson was dressed in a white collared T-shirt and navy-blue slacks, white training shoes. Black knelt down and lifted the T-shirt, exposing Wilson's pale, skinny chest. Bruising on the abdomen and ribs.

Black detected a presence. He turned. Fletcher stood at the doorway, a silhouette in the half dark.

"Is he dead?"

Black nodded. "Well and truly."

Fletcher had regained some of his composure. "Sorry for behaving like a bloody idiot."

"Death affects everybody in different ways. You don't have to apologise to me, Simon."

Fletcher flopped on a chair by the television, and stared at the lifeless form of John Wilson, lying in the centre of the room.

"I can't believe this. He's been a friend for over twenty years. He's about to retire. Everything's going great. Why would he do this?"

"Why does anyone do anything? There's no answer to that. He had it in his mind that this was the only way. And the mind can take you to dark places, if you let it."

"But John Wilson? Surely this can't be happening. I spoke to him only a couple of hours ago."

His voice took on a despondent pitch. "I've never seen a dead body before."

"You get used to the sight, after a while," replied Black. Which was the absolute truth. Black had seen more than his fair share. Death in all its splendour.

"Did he say anything to you? Anything unusual?"

"The whole conversation was unusual. Unreal. And it wasn't really a conversation at all. More like a one-sided rant."

"About what?"

Fletcher gave a long sigh. "Vague stuff. How life had treated him badly. How his life was empty. That he felt neglected in the firm. Unappreciated. Crazy stuff. And that I had to meet him. It didn't sound like the John Wilson I've known for twenty years."

"He wanted to meet you?"

"That's what he said."

"Why would he ask that, when he intended putting a rope round his neck?"

"Jesus, Adam. Tell it like it is." He gazed at Wilson's dead body. "It doesn't make sense."

Black probed further. "But he didn't say anything specific, if any one thing was troubling him?"

Fletcher shook his head.

"Call the police," said Black. "There's nothing more we can do for him now."

He made his way through to a bathroom on the ground floor, and came back with a towel, which he placed over Wilson's face.

His own mobile phone buzzed, a ringing vibration in his jacket pocket. He answered. It was Jennifer. She was trying to keep her voice calm, but it still sounded strained and tight.

"I'm at the house."

Black took a deep breath before he answered. "What's up? Why are you at the house? Are you okay?"

When Jennifer explained what had happened, Black fell silent. There was a sound like a drumbeat in his ears – his heart. At last he spoke, his voice cold.

"You know what to do. I'm leaving now."

24

————

Black asked if he could borrow Fletcher's car, and would have taken it anyway, whatever his response. As it happened, Fletcher was content to wait for the police.

"Go," he said. "The fucking world is falling apart."

And there was a lot of truth in that, Black pondered as he sped from the west end back to Eaglesham, a journey of about fifteen miles. For Black, his world wasn't falling apart – it was being shredded, and all the million parts scattered to the four winds. Only four weeks ago, he had been a hard-working lawyer working in the city, holding down a good job, with a house and a family and everything that was ordinary and made sense. Stress was a transaction going pear-shaped; managing a deadline; a volatile client to handle; or at worst, a call from Jennifer to say Merryn was ill.

Now a call from Jennifer could mean anything. Every time she phoned, his chest seemed to constrict, his heart raced. Stress in the workplace was a mere sideshow attraction compared to the situation now. Once, he had thought that he could handle any shit thrown at him after his experiences in the army. But then he didn't have a wife and child. It was a whole different scenario now. A new and exquisite level of fear. And the gangster known as Peter Grant knew how to turn the screw. He was a connoisseur at this particular game.

But the Special Air Service had gone to exceptional lengths to teach him how to deal with the emotion of fear. Respect it, feel it, embrace it. And once you've accepted that fear itself won't kill you, use it to your advantage. Success and failure are divided by a fine line between those who make fear their friend, and those who choose to make it their enemy. Such was the philosophy of the regiment. *Learn dispassion. Learn objectivity. Become third party.* The SAS were big on mind over emotion. The key to a good soldier was not the brawn but the brain. Or more particularly the mind. Though the knack of knowing how to kill a man was advantageous. Easy when it's you, and only you. Not so easy when those you love are thrust into the theatre of war. Something the SAS had left out of the training manual.

He got to the motorway and hit the gas pedal hard. He sped past turn-offs for Ibrox, Pollok, Paisley, Newton Mearns, finally taking the turn-off for Eaglesham. He would be at his house in ten minutes.

He had killed someone, by sheer fluke, who had the power to wreak revenge from beyond the grave. A gangster's son. What would he have done, he wondered, if the tables were turned – if he had a son, his throat crushed by a stranger in the street, self-defence or otherwise? Might he seek vengeance? He genuinely didn't have an answer. Or perhaps he did, but did not have the courage to admit it.

He pulled up the lane to their house, half expecting to see a top-of-the-range BMW parked in the hammer-head. Instead he saw a blue Ford Mondeo in the driveway behind his wife's car.

He instantly became wary, pulled up adjacent to the house, and made his way to the front door.

He went straight in, and into the living room. Jennifer was

sitting on a corner settee on one side of the room. On the other, on an armchair, was a man he recognised. On the coffee table between them were two envelopes.

The man stood and smiled.

Black responded with a strained smile. "DI Patterson. I believe we've met before."

25

"I called the police," said Jennifer. "After I phoned you. DI Patterson has only just arrived."

"You got here quickly," remarked Black. "I'm impressed." Black sat beside his wife and took her hand.

DI Patterson nodded. "Since our... meeting, I've been assigned your case. When your wife made the call, and we established her name and address, it was automatically referred to me, as the case handler. And when she explained what had happened, I got here pretty fast."

"I'll bet." Black regarded the policeman before him, the man who had questioned him in an interview room only three weeks earlier, suggesting he had links with Glasgow gangland. The man whose manner was now polite and respectful. Today he wasn't wearing glasses, so must have contact lenses in, Black assumed. He was smartly dressed, light-blue suit, blue-and-black-striped tie, little red cufflinks. Lightly tanned. Hair was dark and longer from when Black last remembered it, cut short above the ears, gelled and tousled on top. He was as tall as Black, but leaner, less muscle mass. Black imagined he spent hours on the treadmill, to keep back a middle-age spread so common in policemen. So common in most men, of a certain age.

He switched his attention to the envelopes on the table.

"Are these the letters?"

Jennifer nodded. "I had to come home. I'd forgotten a gift for one of the staff retiring. I got in and saw the two letters on the hall floor. The postman must have delivered them, I guess. And so, I opened them." She took a deep shuddering breath. *Christ,* thought Black, *this is killing her.*

"May I see them?" asked Black, directing his question to DI Patterson.

"I'd rather you didn't. In case of contamination of evidence. Even though Jennifer has touched them, we might still find a fingerprint."

"You're kidding, aren't you? Tell me exactly what's in them."

"They were addressed to me, and... Merryn," replied Jennifer. She hesitated, finding her words. "Two separate letters." She gave a sudden shrill laugh. "At first, when I saw them, I thought they were from the nursery. Maybe an invite to something. The address on the front was handwritten and looked so normal. I could feel that there was something inside but didn't give it any thought. I couldn't have been more wrong."

Black put an arm round her but said nothing.

"I opened the first one, addressed to me, and something fell out..."

She stifled back a sob. Black turned a questioning look towards DI Patterson.

"Each envelope contained a bullet," continued Patterson. "And a note. Not handwritten. Typed. Each identical."

"What did the notes say?"

Patterson gave Black a long stare. When he spoke, the words struck Black to the soul.

"*The next one has your name on it.*"

Two bullets. One for Jennifer, one for Merryn, their purpose clear and unequivocal.

Peter Grant wasn't finished. Not by a long way.

26

"So, what now?" asked Black.

DI Patterson lifted a leather briefcase sitting at his feet, and placed it on his knees. He opened it. Inside was a file, a notepad, pens placed neatly in a row in pen holders, a pair of forensic gloves, and some transparent polythene sample bags.

"With both your consent, I would like to take this back to the station, to have them analysed. We can check for prints, postmark, maybe even check the paper used. Also, every bullet has a serial number, normally, so this can give us a good idea about their source, where they were made."

"These ones won't, I can assure you," said Black. "They'll have been specially made. Bespoke, one might say. Built in someone's garage or workshop or basement. But sure, take them away."

Jennifer nodded.

Patterson put on the gloves, reopened the letters, and picked out the bullet from each one.

"Can you show me, please?" asked Black.

"Of course." Patterson held one up, balancing it between thumb and index finger.

Black recognised it immediately. A 7.62mm calibre. Standard issue for Special Services. Bigger than the normal calibre issued to the regular army. Affectionately known as a one-shot kill. Practically eviscerates the target. Black had used many such rounds over the years. When Black fired a weapon, he liked the guarantee of death, and this bullet never failed. Peter Grant knew exactly what he was doing.

"Do you know your bullets, Mr Black?" enquired Patterson.

"I've had some experience. Over the years."

Patterson put it in an evidence bag, sealed it, wrote a number on the label, and repeated the process for each item – two bullets, two letters, two envelopes – and put the bags in his briefcase.

He then took a brief statement from Jennifer, who recounted what she had already told him, which was not a lot, and put the notepad in the briefcase as well. He clicked it shut.

"So, what now?" said Black, repeating his initial question.

DI Patterson regarded him with a quizzical stare. "As I've said, Mr Black, we'll get the stuff analysed…"

"That's not what my husband means," Jennifer snapped. "You're not obtuse! This is not rocket science. You need to tell us what the hell you're going to do about it. It's not as if you don't know the history here. You kept my husband at the police station long enough. You know the bullets were sent by Peter Grant. Or someone in his fucking *organisation,* or whatever you call his gang. You know he did. And I have a four-year-old daughter to think about. And these fucking animals have just sent her a fucking bullet. So, we're asking you, for the third time – what the fuck happens now?"

Couldn't have put it better myself, thought Black.

Patterson shifted uncomfortably. "Of course, it's supposition. We don't have any tangible evidence to connect Grant with this. At least at this stage. But once we've analysed–"

"So, who do you think sent the bullets," Jennifer broke in again, "the fucking milkman, because we didn't pay last week's milk? Please don't treat us like idiots. We need protection. We need help!"

"Do you have CCTV?"

"No, but we can get it," said Black. "But what about a police presence. A police officer – stationed at the foot of the lane, for example."

Patterson shook his head. "I'm not trying to be obstructive, but there's no way we could stretch to that. Cuts and savings. We don't have the money or resources. I can arrange for a drive-by at least once a day. And I can arrange for your alarm to be upgraded, so that we get a distress signal at the station as soon as you hit a panic button."

"A panic button," repeated Black. "Big deal. That's a real comfort. What about a witness protection programme? We're not witnesses, but targets. Surely something can be arranged?"

"You said it yourself," replied Patterson. "You're not witnesses. Something like that won't be sanctioned by the Crown Office unless there's an ongoing prosecution. Which there's not."

He shifted again, not looking at them. "There is something you could consider. Though you might not like the suggestion."

They waited for him to speak, but Black had a good idea what was about to be said.

Patterson took a deep breath. "Have you considered moving? To give yourself some distance? Maybe to another part of the country, perhaps?"

"And that's a serious suggestion?" retorted Jennifer. "You're asking us to turn tail and hide away from a psychopath, rather than have the hassle of dealing with the psychopath yourself. I can't believe I'm hearing this. This is fucking unbelievable!"

"It wouldn't make a difference," said Black in a hollow voice.

"It doesn't matter the distance." *Blood for blood,* thought Black. Peter Grant was the type of man who would demand his pound of flesh. And then some.

Patterson stood. "I understand how you must feel. But until Peter Grant actually does something we can tie him to, then we're in limbo."

Black gave him a fixed stare. "You can't possibly understand how we feel. Unless this is taken to Grant, he's going to take it to us. That's the way this is going to play."

~

Black saw Patterson out.

"I take it I'm no longer a suspect," said Black, as they stood at the doorway.

Patterson appraised Black for a few seconds before he spoke. "It so happened there was a CCTV camera at the doorway of the pub. And as luck would have it, it was turned on when the incident took place. The whole thing is recorded. I saw what happened that night in Eaglesham. From start to finish. I saw what you did to these men, with your bare hands. They attacked the wrong man. And in doing so, two of them met a swift end. I have no complaints. Case closed."

"Good to hear," replied Black. "One less thing to worry about. I know there's only so much you can do but keep an eye out. For my family. Please."

Patterson nodded. "You're on my watch."

27

Time passed. Several weeks.

Nathan Grant was supposed to meet the contract killer known simply as Joshua, at the prearranged rendezvous and at the prearranged time – the Hilton Hotel off Byres Road, in the west end of Glasgow, at noon. Chosen by him. When he arrived in the foyer, he got a call from Joshua on his mobile, to say the meeting place had changed. That it was now the Four Oaks Hotel in Perth, and that they should meet in ninety minutes. He would be carrying a wine-red leather briefcase.

Nathan was unimpressed and swore under his breath. But orders were orders. And he was dealing with an individual whose profession demanded caution, bordering on paranoia.

The drive took an hour and fifteen minutes – a sixty-mile journey. The Four Oaks Hotel sat overlooking the River Tay: a solid, squat, nondescript building with a drab grey frontage, built a hundred years ago, unremarkable from any other, and nowhere near as plush as the Hilton.

The reception area was small and manned by two staff. Through double glass doors were the bar and lounge. It was busier than Nathan had expected. People were having lunch at tables, and others were sitting at the bar on high stools. Cheap food and cheap booze, he thought. Pub fare. Easy to blend in and become invisible. A man was sitting at a small table by a window reading a newspaper. His face was hidden. On the table was a pot of tea and a cup and saucer, and on the chair opposite him was a slim red briefcase with gold-coloured combination locks.

Nathan approached him, manoeuvring past people eating and drinking and engrossed in conversation. No one paid him any attention.

"Joshua?"

The man lowered his newspaper.

Nathan saw a man with bland, tired features; blond thinning hair; sallow complexion. Clean-shaven. Perhaps forty-five, though difficult to tell. He looked like any typical office worker you'd see in a thousand offices anywhere. Forgettable. Invisible. He was dressed like half the people in the room. Cheap dark suit, tie, white shirt.

"Sit, please."

Nathan removed the briefcase and placed it carefully on the floor and sat opposite him.

"Would you care for a cup of tea? Or coffee perhaps?" He spoke softly, with no accent, but firmly, every word clipped and concise. A bit like airline pilots, when they're speaking to passengers through the intercom.

"Coffee, thanks. White. No sugar."

The man known as Joshua beckoned a waiter over, and gave him the order, asking for a fresh cup of tea for himself. And some extra milk.

"It's good to meet you, at last," said Nathan. "A last-minute change of venue?"

"You could say that. Predictability can be tiresome. I like to surprise. Don't you? And anyway, the food is far too expensive in those fancy hotels, don't you think? A place like this is more reasonable for simple tastes. Food and drink for the common man."

"You have simple tastes?"

"Generally."

"Was the transfer successful?" Nathan had the previous day transferred one million euros to a Paris bank from one of the several companies they controlled from the Cayman Islands. Not such simple tastes, really.

"The transfer was absolutely fine. No delays at the airport, for a pleasant change."

"That's good. So now you're here, you'll be visiting soon, we all hope."

"You're very hospitable. I intend to be visiting briefly. Tomorrow. And then straight home."

The waiter returned with a tray of tea and coffee, and a side plate of shortbread, which he placed on the table between them, removing the used pot and cup. Joshua thanked him.

The conversation stopped as Joshua poured milk into his cup, gave the teapot a stir, then poured in the tea.

"Shortbread?"

"No thanks," said Nathan.

"Me neither. Too rich. I must watch what I eat. The slightest thing gives me heartburn, which isn't pleasant if you've ever had it. Acid reflux is what I think it's called. It's the sugar which causes it, so the experts say."

"I don't get heartburn," replied Nathan. "I just get fat."

"You look trim. You must work out."

Nathan responded with the merest of shrugs. "I try. In our line of work, we have to keep fit, I suppose. You know how it is."

Joshua nodded. "I do. I ought to get to the gym more often. But I never seem to get the time. Or perhaps I don't have the inclination. I find the task boring, pushing weights about, or cycling on a machine and ending up nowhere. It takes commitment. Something I must lack, sadly."

Another sip of tea.

"You're visiting tomorrow then?" asked Nathan.

"Yes. Most definitely. But not for long. In fact, it'll be a swift hello, a swift goodbye. And then off."

"A swift goodbye. You have all the details?"

"Thank you, yes. You've been most thorough in your directions."

"And you've made all the preparations?"

Joshua's lips twitched into the semblance of a smile. "You don't need to concern yourself with all the small print. When I visit, I like to plan things to a meticulous detail. I am, shall we say, ruthless about minutiae. Fastidious, one might say. I like things to run smoothly. One can never plan too much. And you've been most obliging with all the information you've given me. Extremely useful. I always research a place well before a visit. It makes the whole trip that bit more fun, don't you think? Immersing yourself in the history, the geography, the culture, the people."

"I suppose it does. Of course, if you get lost, or need assistance, then I'm only a phone call away. We're here to help."

"That's very reassuring. Can you help with the weather? The times I've visited, it feels like I've arrived in the Arctic. Not that I've visited the Arctic before. I don't know how you survive."

"I don't." Nathan laughed. "I wake up to a shitty day like this and wonder seriously why God would make a place like Scotland."

"To torment you. Or perhaps to test you. I've never put much store in God, personally. It is what it is, and life goes on."

"Or doesn't."

Joshua acknowledged the comment with the slightest nod, raising his teacup. "As the case may be."

~

Nathan pressed speed dial on his mobile phone and within seconds got through to Grant.

"I met him," said Nathan. "Gives me the creeps, to be honest."

"At the price he charges," Grant replied, "I should fucking hope so. When?"

"He says tomorrow."

"So be it. It can't come too soon. He didn't need anything?"

"He says he's prepared. And I believe him."

"Tomorrow then. Tomorrow I get my life back. And Adam Black's new life begins." Grant hung up.

Nathan got into his car, parked a hundred yards from the hotel, in a side street. He had a bad feeling about this, but he had chosen not to mention it to his uncle, because he simply didn't have the courage to question anything Peter Grant did. But his gut told him this was bad – that there would be consequences. He thought about Jimmy, blinded in one eye. He thought about Damian and the Manchester hardman William Blakely, both cold in their coffins, and Teacup, ex-boxer, out of hospital, still struggling for coordination in his arms and legs, and Nathan shuddered, and not with the winter's cold.

Maybe, just maybe, they were picking the wrong fight with the wrong man.

28

Six weeks had passed since the bullet message.

Six weeks to the day.

The funeral of John Wilson had taken place during this time; a sombre affair. He was Catholic, though not practising. Black had no idea. He had been working closely with the man for five years and had no clue about his religion. It just never came up, wasn't relevant. Black didn't give a damn either way. The church was half-full – a smattering of relatives; a fairly large contingent of golfing buddies who all actually looked as if they were going straight from the church to the first tee; a distraught girlfriend dressed dramatically in black, sobbing quietly behind a dark gauze veil – Black learned she had been seeing Wilson for all of four weeks prior to his death. Gold-digger, Fletcher had suggested. Black had no views on the matter. His only son had flown from Melbourne, Australia, where he was doing well as a real estate agent.

And of course, there was Simon Fletcher and himself, and some other lawyers, old friends and sparring partners, there to pay their respects to a colleague who had endured the hustle and bustle of the law for over forty years.

The day had been cold and grey, the sun hidden by low unbroken cloud.

His coffin was lowered into the ground, the church softening its stance on suicides buried in a Catholic cemetery, no longer regarded as a mortal sin. Black and Fletcher had helped to lower it on white silken cord. The priest had spoken some short words, a final prayer. The service had ended.

The reception had been held at a sectioned off area of a trendy bistro/bar called the Green Dolphin in the west end – the entire ground floor of a one-hundred-year-old building. Buffet food was made available in heated silver trays. Conversation had been muted and sad. The mood strained. Difficult for people to deal with this type of death, Black thought. So many unanswered questions. Mixed emotions; confusion, guilt, sorrow. Fletcher and Black remained at the bar, each with a whisky and ice, pondering the loss of their friend.

"I can't believe the old bugger's gone," Fletcher said. The coroner had confirmed what they already knew. Death by suicide. Asphyxiation. "What a way to exit. It's impossible to take in. What the hell is wrong with this world?" Fletcher gazed at the honey-gold liquid in his glass, his voice barely above a whisper. "Why would he do such a thing?"

It was a rhetorical question, but Black chose to answer anyway.

"We'll probably never know what happened."

Fletcher cocked his head, regarding him quizzically. "How do you mean?"

Black kept his thoughts to himself.

During those six weeks, they went about their lives, sticking to routines, not going out. DI Patterson kept in touch. He updated

Black with the forensic results of the bullets, and the letters. As Black had predicted, nothing was found. The bullets had no serial number. There were no fingerprints; the paper was the type used in a million places; the handwriting could have been anyone's; the printing used in each letter was impossible to source. A complete blank. Black had expected nothing more.

Every day, occasionally twice a day, a police constable would pay a visit, checking up, ensuring all was well. Patterson was doing his best, reflected Black. For that he was grateful.

Black had got a call on his mobile one Friday afternoon. From DI Patterson. "Fancy a drink?" he'd asked.

Black met Patterson in a pub called the Red Serpent, in a cobbled lane close to Glasgow Queen Street railway station, almost plumb centre in the city, two hundred yards from Black's office. The place was long and narrow and quiet, the light muted. Nothing gaudy. Low-key. High stools at the bar, and rows of booths against one wall. Men sat quietly on their own, reading newspapers, or staring at nothing in particular, as they contemplated their next drink. A group were playing dominoes in a corner. A dartboard was fixed on a wall. A drinker's pub. Despite the smoking ban, the place still smelled of stale cigarettes.

Patterson was sitting at one of the high stools, a glass of whisky on the bar in front of him. He waved Black to the seat next to him.

"What's your poison?"

"Glenfiddich goes down rather well. Neat."

"Couldn't agree with you more."

Patterson ordered two drinks. Black sat on the high stool next to him.

"Thanks for coming. Especially at such short notice."

Black shrugged. "No problem. But I can't stay long. You understand why."

Patterson nodded. "Understood."

The barman placed two drinks on the bar. Patterson raised his glass. "To catching the bad guys."

Black clinked his glass. "Here's hoping. Why the drink? Without meaning to be blunt, I assume something's happened?"

Patterson sipped the whisky. "Nothing's happened. The drink is an apology. An olive branch? We read you wrong, that night. Turned out you were on the side of right, and those three bastards picked the wrong man."

"The side of right," repeated Black quietly. "I'm not sure about that. Two of those bastards ended up dead."

"In my book, exactly where they belong."

"Some might argue differently."

Patterson hovered the whisky under his nose, took another sip. "You have skills. I watched the CCTV replay. I've never seen anything like it. Where did you learn to fight like that?"

"I was in the army for many years. You pick stuff up. Don't be too impressed. Look where it's got me."

"You're alive," said Patterson. "You could be dead. I'm Colin, by the way."

Black took a drink of the Glenfiddich, let the liquid rest on his tongue. His favourite whisky. He had always been sure to take a bottle with him in all the countries he'd been sent to. A little taste of home.

"Imagine," continued Patterson. "A guy like Damian Grant being in Eaglesham, and running into someone like you. How random is that?"

"As random as it gets. Some might describe it as less random, more bad luck."

"For them."

"For us," said Black. "For my family. Make no mistake. Peter Grant won't let this go."

"It's been weeks. A man like Grant is all bluster. I've been in the job long enough to know that these people will only take it so far. He wants to scare you, sure. But that's as far as this'll go. He knows if he tries anything, we'll be on him quicker than shit off a shoe. I've got a uniform coming to your house every day. If there's even the slightest worry in your mind, then phone me directly." He fished out his wallet, pulled out a card, gave it to Black. "This has got my direct number. You phone any time."

Black nodded, and took another drink. But he had a gut feeling. He could be handed every card by every DI in the country, and it still wouldn't be enough. A man like Peter Grant was an unstoppable force. He'd come again, and again. Him and his gang. Forever.

"Cut the head off the snake," Black said idly. "Perhaps it's the only way."

"Let us do our job, Adam. He's not above the law." He regarded Black solemnly. "And neither are you. Keep remembering – he's just another fucking hoodlum in a nice suit. He makes one wrong move, and we'll get him. No problem. That, I promise."

Black gave a cold smile. "You promise?"

"You bet."

The days grew into weeks. It seemed a degree of normality was seeping into their lives. Jennifer appeared less fearful, didn't glance over her shoulder as often. At least it looked like that on the outside.

"Maybe it's over," she would whisper to him at night-time, in the morning, if they were in the car, if they were watching television in the evening, having dinner. "Maybe nothing's going to happen."

"Could be," Black would reply. But he was less optimistic,

and kept vigilant, his guard never down, his nerves stretched almost on an hourly basis, watching for the slightest signs, anything at all out of the ordinary. Or anything ordinary. A trip to the shops, emptying the bins, filling petrol in the car. Waking in the morning. Every action, however mundane, tinged with jeopardy. When his mobile phone rang, he took a deep breath before he answered. He played everything down. He went to work, he came home.

He waited.

Exactly six weeks had passed since the bullet message. The beginning of March.

It was a day like no other.

It was the day Adam Black's world changed.

29

Black, Jennifer and Merryn left the house together at seven forty-five. It was a Tuesday. The mornings and early evenings were still dark. It was bitter cold. Winter kept its grip; the grass, the pavements, car roofs and windscreens coated in a veneer of frost. Like sugar coating. They took separate cars. Black, initially, had been their constant chaperone. Jennifer, with a fierce determination, had said no. It had to stop. They needed normality. She would not allow their lives to be changed. Had insisted on it. Demanded it. Black, grudgingly, relented.

Black went straight to work. Jennifer, with Merryn strapped to a child's safety seat in the back, drove her Range Rover Discovery to a local nursery based in the civic hall in the centre of Eaglesham, dropped her off, and then made the journey to the Royal Alexandra hospital in Paisley, a twelve-mile drive. Traffic was solid. It took longer than usual. She listened to the radio, then a CD. Sixties music. Rock 'n' roll. The classics.

The day was frantic, as ever. Every two minutes, something happening. The day cluttered with minor emergencies. She was a consultant in the paediatric unit. Everybody wanted something all the time. Reports, meetings, diagnoses, answers.

Constant. But at that moment in her life, it was an antidote. A temporary cure for the shitstorm looming on the horizon.

Jennifer worked part-time. She stopped at 2.15pm, as usual. Sometimes she was later, but rarely. She drove straight back to the nursery, to pick her daughter up for 3pm, lingered for a chat with other mums, and then drove straight home. Sometimes she stopped off at the supermarket en route, sometimes the park, to let Merryn play on the swings with other kids. But not today. She arrived back at the house at about 3.30pm. Black would be home by 4.30, having drastically reduced his hours, doubtless carrying a box-load of files.

She got into the front hallway, closed the door behind her. The alarm immediately beeped. The first thing she did was switch the central heating timer to *on*. Old houses were cold houses. It was freezing. Double glazing didn't help. The walls were thick, but winter still creeped in. Next, she punched in a code, switching the alarm to *off*. The beeping was silenced. A brand new system, every space in the house covered. A direct link to the police. A mouse couldn't get in, and if it did, the place was lit up like the Fourth of July. Merryn went immediately through to the lounge, to sit on a beanbag, brightly coloured with blue and red hearts and smiling teddy bears.

Jennifer switched the television on, finding the kids channel. She made her way to the kitchen, to think about dinner. She opened the fridge, and took out a bottle of white wine. The bottle was a quarter full. The remnants of the previous evening. She opened it, poured herself a glass. The doorbell rang. She went back to the hallway, expecting to see the blurred image of a police constable through the marbled glass of the front door. Which was exactly what she saw. It was a regular thing for the police to check up on them at this time, courtesy of DI Patterson. And every time it happened, she gave him a silent *thank you*. She double-checked, glancing at an image on a small screen on a table by the door, relayed from a CCTV camera installed in a corner of the porch outside. A single policeman.

She unlocked the door, opened it.

The policeman smiled. "Mrs Black?"

"Everything's fine, thank you," she said, returning the smile.

"Glad to hear it. There's been a development. A very positive one. May I come in?"

"Of course."

He entered, taking off his hat. He was average height, average build. A careworn face. Thin, wispy hair. "Sorry to trouble you, Mrs. Black. But I have some good news."

Her heart lifted. She had no idea what he was about to say. But it sounded like what she needed to hear. She would take anything even vaguely like *good*. "Would you like a cup of tea, or a coffee perhaps?"

He seemed to hesitate.

"Please," she urged. "It's freezing out there. If you've got news, and it's nice news, then at least let's share a drink." She laughed. "Though I'm having a glass of wine, if that's okay."

"Sounds perfectly reasonable to me," he said. "A cup of tea? Why not. Five minutes won't kill anybody."

"Of course it won't."

He followed her through the hallway, into the kitchen, at the back of the house. The door to the living room was open. Merryn was sitting on her oversized beanbag, in front of the television, her back to the door, captivated by the cartoon channel.

"Your daughter?"

"Yes," said Jennifer. "Four years old, and addicted to daytime television."

The policeman laughed. "I remember those days. Mine's grown up, and flown the coop. You miss them, when they go."

His face broke into a broad grin. "For a few minutes. Then you appreciate the tranquillity."

She filled the kettle, switched it on. "You have a daughter?"

"She's thirty. Graduated in law. Working for some fancy firm."

"Well done her. My husband's a lawyer."

"It's something I would like to have tried. Never got the qualifications. Didn't stick it at school. For my sins, I joined the police force. Here I am."

"For your sins? You guys do a fantastic job."

The policeman placed his hat on the kitchen counter. He made a show of looking about. A pause. "You have a lovely house."

Jennifer shrugged. "It wasn't like this when we bought it. A complete mess. A lot of time, a lot of money." She showed a brief wintry smile. "And a lot of tears."

"Worthwhile tears," said the policeman. "You have something to show for it. Something tangible. Bricks and mortar. A lovely family. Nice car. All the trappings. You know something I don't understand?"

"What?"

"Why people shed needless tears."

"Sorry?"

"For example, why shed tears for the dead?"

Jennifer frowned. "I don't follow you."

The policeman gave a crooked grin. "It's like crying over spilt milk. It serves no practical purpose. A wasted effort. You know what I say, Jennifer?"

Her heart skipped a beat. First name? The conversation wasn't right. Far from it.

She answered, her voice strained. "What do you say?"

"Who cares? The dead don't matter. The dead can rot in the ground. My name's Joshua, by the way."

The kettle clicked.

She opened a cupboard door, got a mug, placed it slowly on the counter, heart racing.

"What do you say, Jennifer? Am I right?"

"What do you take?" she asked, not answering, her back to him. She swallowed. In the room next door was her four-year-old daughter.

"I've changed my mind. I don't want tea. Sorry for the inconvenience. I don't really have time."

She took a deep breath. She turned. He was leaning back on the kitchen worktop. She cleared her throat, kept her voice calm. "My husband will be back any minute. You said you had good news?"

He shook his head. "Nice try, Jennifer. I admire your composure. Your husband isn't due back for what – forty-five minutes? If it's any consolation, that is exactly what I would have said, if I were in your position. My compliments, for quick thinking, under pressure."

"What do you want?" She could hardly speak the words. Her throat felt constricted.

He raised an eyebrow, the corners of his mouth drooping. "As I mentioned. To give you good news."

She waited. Time had frozen. Her entire world revolved round this one moment.

"Your worries are all over," he said softly. "You can rest now. You and your daughter. Endless peace. I wonder if Adam will shed tears."

His voice dropped to a whisper. "*Bonne nuit.*"

She stood, transfixed. She raised one hand, tried to say something. Tried to plead.

He pulled out a revolver from a pocket in his coat, equipped with a silencer, almost as if in slow motion, and from three yards, shot her twice in the face, in rapid succession. Each shot was muffled, like a cushion being punched.

He shot again, where she lay.

He stepped over her, made his way into the living room.

Three more muffled shots.

The beanbag's bright colours became one.

Five seconds later he left, closing the front door quietly behind him.

30

The police arrived – a blazing convoy. Two ambulances. Vans, cars. A helicopter buzzed high above. Police marksmen prepared themselves. But the killer had long departed. What they found was Black sitting on the floor of his lounge.

On one side, her head cradled on his lap, was the body of his wife. On the other was the tiny body of his daughter. They lay next to him, outstretched, as if using his lap as a pillow.

They could have been sleeping. But they were dead. Their faces were gone. Their blood mingled, soaked the ground, creating a dark stain on the carpet.

Black stared ahead, but his gaze was inward. The world no longer existed. Nothing mattered. He had lived with death all his life. Death had lived with him. It was part of him, like a cancer. He looked inward and saw his soul. It was broken with the blood of those he loved. This was on him.

And the man called Peter Grant.

More blood would spill. Lots.

Grant was a dead man walking.

31

Peter Grant was told about the event in the Black household long before it made the news. In fact, he was informed ten minutes after it happened. He was sitting in the back conservatory of his suburban mansion. He was alone. Thor, his constant shadow, was in another part of the house. This was a moment too special to share with anyone. Grant was sitting in the same chair that the chief constable had been sitting in only weeks ago, when he was divulging the history of Adam Black's life.

Grant gazed out at his magnificent gardens, at the delicate and perfect Japanese moon bridge, the still water over which it spanned. It was a clear, crisp afternoon, the sky pale blue in the frosty sunshine. But Grant was not appreciating the view at that precise moment. His mind was fixed on other things.

His mobile phone, resting on the arm of his seat, vibrated. It was his nephew, Nathan.

Grant didn't answer it immediately. He wanted to savour this moment. He wanted to live it a thousand times over. This was a moment he knew he would look back on and remember for the rest of his days.

He picked up.

"It's done."

Grant disconnected.

He never drank alcohol. He hated the weakness of those who did. He'd seen too many lives ruined and broken. He hadn't touched a drop for twenty-five years. But sometimes rules had to be broken, exceptions made.

On the low coffee table in front of him was the file on Adam Black. On top of it was a crystal glass of whisky, neat. Chivas Regal. Grant stretched over, picked it up, let it hover under his nose. He raised the glass before him, as if toasting an invisible friend, and watched the whisky gleam like liquid gold as it caught the sun.

"Here's to you, Captain Black. May your family rot in hell."

He took a sip and placed the glass back on top of the file.

He picked up his mobile and pressed a number.

A voice answered, almost immediately.

"I want it done," said Grant. "Fourteen days tops. The money will be deposited next week. I'll see to it personally. Abacus is ready. Then we can tie things up. Do you foresee any problems at your end?"

The voice responded.

"What about Black?" said Grant.

The voice again.

"I don't believe in random chance," said Grant. "He killed Damian to get to me. We have to assume this. That he planned it. The man who doesn't anticipate every play is a fucking dead man. We'll kill him, and feed his heart to the worms."

The voice again.

"Fourteen days, maximum," replied Grant. "Then you can start enjoying life a little."

He put the phone down.

Back to business, he thought. He would keep Black on the backburner for a short while, to make him feel it. Feel the despair and sorrow. The pain.

And after that, Grant would do what he did best.

He would erase Adam Black's existence.

32

Black was gently ushered into the back of a police car, escorted by two policemen. He watched as a team of forensic scientists, garbed from head to foot in their white papery-plastic suits, entered his house, filing through the porch door, one at a time.

Don't wake them, he thought. *They're sleeping.*

Tape was used to cordon off the crime scene. Policemen and women, some in uniform and some not, spoke in little huddles, occasionally darting a glance towards Black. He didn't care. Strangers occupied his house. White plastic screening was erected around the porch.

The police car he was in drove off. Jennifer and Merryn were gone, forever. Their existence wiped clean. The sum and total of their lives reduced to nothing.

They drove back to the main police station based in Pitt Street, Glasgow city centre. He felt as if he were in a strange waking dream. One part of him was in it, experiencing every moment, another part was watching from a distance, a dispassionate observer.

He was asked to remove his clothing – he was covered in his

family's blood. He was given trousers, T-shirt, sandals. The part of his mind which watched remembered having done this before, not so long ago. He was asked some questions:

We're so sorry about your loss, Mr Black. Can you tell us what happened?

I came home from work. Just before five. I opened the door. A pause, as he summoned up the strength to articulate the scene he had confronted. *I saw my wife lying on the kitchen floor. I went through to the living room. My daughter was lying beside the television. I went back to the kitchen, to Jennifer, lifted her. She was so light. Like carrying nothing at all. I carried her to living room. I wanted all of us to be together. A last goodbye. I phoned the police. You came. I'm here.*

Did you see anyone?

No.

He was asked if there was anywhere he could go.

Phone Simon Fletcher. I can maybe stay with him. Black had no family. An orphan. Brother long dead. No relatives as far as he knew. Except Jennifer's mother, who at this moment would still be unaware that her only daughter and granddaughter were lying dead with bullets in their head. He dreaded the moment when he would need to make that call.

Check the CCTV, he mumbled. *We have one at the front. You might get a face.*

We know, Mr Black. We're checking everything.

Thank you.

Simon Fletcher arrived fifteen minutes later. Their office was a short drive from the station. Nothing was said. They drove back to Fletcher's house. A converted four-bedroomed Georgian sandstone flat in the Pollokshields area of Glasgow. High ceilings with ornate cornicing, stained-glass windows and candelabra-style lighting in every room.

"Stay as long as you want," said Fletcher, as they sat in the car outside. "I don't know what to say, Adam. I can't believe this is happening."

"Believe it," said Adam, in a flat, lifeless monotone. "It's happening."

33

Black stayed with Simon Fletcher. Fletcher was married with two daughters, eleven and twelve. There was a spare room for him. His wife – Adele – was French, born in Bordeaux, moved to Scotland fifteen years previously and who spoke English fluently. The family cried when they heard what happened. Fletcher went to work every day, contacted Black's clients, made arrangements to delay, cancel, adjust, all with the assistance of the five paralegals who worked for the firm. All of them capable. He was allowed to get some things for Black from the house – clothes mainly. Black vowed he would never go back.

On the fourth day after the murders, Black was asked back to Pitt Street police station. There was an update, and he might be interested.

He was taken to an office. A uniformed officer was sitting behind a desk. He stood as soon as Black was shown in. He was a big man, about the same height as Black. Iron-grey hair, shaved to the bone at the sides, thick bull neck, square-jawed, steady pale-blue eyes, wide shoulders.

He looked directly at Adam when he spoke, his eyes clear

and candid. This was not a man to shy away from awkward situations.

"Please accept my condolences, Mr Black. My name is Chief Inspector Francis Starling. I'll be the case co-ordinator, so if you've any questions I'll be happy to answer them, if I can."

Black nodded and sat. The office was utilitarian at best. There were a couple of shelves on one wall holding rows of thick ring binder files with numbers written on the spines. On another wall was a photograph of the chief inspector being awarded with a prize of some sort. The desk was clear with the exception of a laptop and a phone, and a tray of letters. The window behind him had bars on it and offered a view of a car park.

"Case co-ordinator?" replied Black.

Starling gave a small half-smile. "It's new police speak – I'm in charge, is what it means. Tea or coffee?"

Black shook his head. "You asked to see me? Have you caught the killer?" Black of course knew the answer already.

"Not yet. But we're not leaving any stone unturned. I hope this doesn't cause offence, but we've got a copy of the CCTV footage outside your door – when the... incident took place. I wonder if I could show you some stills taken from the footage. Of the man who we're pretty sure carried out the attack. In case you recognise him? Maybe you've seen him somewhere before? It's a big ask. If you want to walk right back out the door, then that's okay with me."

"Show me."

Starling opened a drawer in his desk and pulled out an A3-sized plain brown envelope. He opened it and placed three photographs in front of Black, as if he were dealing cards. Black looked at the photos, almost in a state of wonder – there was the man who had murdered his family!

The quality was good. He saw a profile of a white male,

nondescript face, unremarkable features, the hair covered by a peaked cap, the type worn by policemen. A face difficult to remember. No distinguishing marks. A lot of people were bad with faces, good with names. Black was excellent with faces. This particular one was now branded into his memory.

"Have you seen this man before?"

"Never."

"You're sure?"

"Positive."

"You'll see he's wearing a police uniform, standard issue, right down to the police identification number on the epaulettes, which is false."

"He doesn't care," said Black.

"Come again?"

"He would have known about the camera. He would have known everything about our surveillance system. He's a careful, disciplined man. Yet he made no effort to cover his face. My guess he got a vast amount of money to do this, so this is his last job. He'll disappear to some obscure part of the world where he can live his life as a ghost, and you'll never see him again. And by keeping his face uncovered, he's also sending a message."

"What message is that, Mr Black?"

"That whoever's behind this is above the law. That he's untouchable, and he knows it. And he wants us to know it. A display of arrogance."

"That might be one way of looking at it. But things like that don't tend to happen. We've seen many terrible things, Mr Black, and usually it comes down to something as simple as someone with a grudge. You're a lawyer, aren't you? I was hoping you might have recognised him as a disgruntled client? Someone your firm might have represented in the past? Someone who thinks you owe them?"

Black held Starling's stare for an uncomfortably long time. He could hardly believe he was hearing this.

"You know there's a history here."

Starling gave a placatory smile. "We're well aware of what happened to Mr Grant's son–"

"Mr Grant?" interrupted Black. "Okay. So, there's only one person in this entire world who feels he's owed. And that's Peter Grant. And you know exactly who Peter Grant is. This is not a complex calculus theory. You get it, surely."

"We shouldn't jump to conclusions, Mr Black. There's absolutely nothing to connect Peter Grant to what happened here."

"Except basic logic. Grant's son died. He thinks I'm to blame. Nine weeks later, my wife and child are shot by an assassin. And it so happens that Peter Grant is the head of the Scottish equivalent of the Mafia. Where am I going wrong here? And of course, there's the bullets."

Starling cocked his head. "What bullets?"

Black hesitated. A sudden thought struck him. "Can I speak to DI Patterson? He was my case handler."

Starling took a deep breath. "That would be impossible."

"Why?"

Starling held his stare for a full five seconds.

"DI Colin Patterson is dead."

Black waited.

"He was involved in a car crash two days ago." He lowered his voice. "His car skidded off the road. A tragic accident. He died at the scene. Did you know him well?"

Black absorbed the information. The conclusion reached in his mind was chilling. "Well enough."

"You mentioned bullets?" continued Starling.

"It's nothing, sorry. I'm just a little confused with everything that's happened. No, I'm not aware of any disgruntled clients. And I don't recognise the man in the picture."

"All right, Mr Black. Thank you for your assistance during this terrible time. Once again, I would like to extend my condolences. If you can think of anything at all, anything, then please get in touch. No stone will be left unturned. Let me assure you."

He reached into the same drawer he got the photographs from and gave Black a card.

"This is the number for Victim Support. Telephone them day or night. They'll listen and give you guidance through this trying time."

They shook hands. Black was escorted back out of the building. The first thing he did was toss the card he had been given into a rubbish bin. Black was no victim.

No stone will be left unturned. Patterson was dead. The police didn't know about the bullets.

Black was on his own.

Which suited him just fine.

But first things first. He needed to talk things through. And he knew who to talk to.

The padre.

34

Peter Grant spent every fourth weekend in his 'hunting cabin'. He didn't partake in any hunting as such, save the occasional grouse shoot. But that's how he liked to describe his mountain retreat. It wasn't a cabin either – it was a sprawling eight-bedroomed logwood alpine mansion, equipped with gym, sauna and a twenty-seat cinema room, with a separate guest house set in the grounds. Built in a thousand acres of prime forestland in the heart of the Scottish Highlands, it overlooked the pure blue waters of Loch Morlich, with an unspoiled view of the snow-topped Cairngorms.

The weekend following the murders, Grant decided a visit to the cabin was deserved. He arrived early on a crisp Saturday morning accompanied by Thor, Nathan and several other members of his entourage, having all driven up the two-and-a-half-hour journey in three Range Rovers. When Grant got out the car, he gazed at the row of mountains, vast and sheer, only two miles distant, and took a deep lungful of the zesty, pine-fresh mountain air.

The nation had been shocked by the crime. Grant was pleased. You fuck with Peter Grant, then you fuck with the devil himself. A vengeful devil. He felt uplifted. A burden had been removed. His son's death had been avenged.

"Look upon that view," he said to Nathan. He was in an expansive mood. "Where else can you open your front door and see a spectacle like that. Only in Scotland."

"Not in the east end of Glasgow, for sure," Nathan replied, giving a sardonic smile.

"Hear that, Thor!" shouted Grant. "You got mountains like that in Berlin?"

Thor, in loose sweat top and baggy jogging trousers, was taking luggage out the car. He glanced round, a puzzled look on his face.

"Forget it," said Grant. "Fucking imbecile," he muttered to Nathan. "All muscles and no grey matter. But I guess I don't pay them for their stunning IQ."

His phone buzzed. It was a call he was expecting. Chief Constable Mathew Smith.

"Yes, Mathew."

Mathew Smith launched straight in.

"Your man went to the house as a fucking policeman?" During all their many chats, this was the first time Grant had heard the chief constable swear. Grant wasn't in the least bit fazed.

"Good to hear from you too."

"As a policeman? When this gets out – and it most surely will – the publicity will crucify us, and I kid you not. Did you ever stop to think about repercussions? What about the media? What are the public going to think? Let me answer that for you – they'll think there's a fucking homicidal rogue cop out there killing women and children. Because that's how it's going to look!"

Grant couldn't help grinning. "You deny, of course. And you tell the truth. He was disguised. That's all there is to it."

"But it's public perception. People will think it really was a copper, and the whole thing is one big fucking cover-up! Yet another conspiracy theory! And the fallout will be massive, make no mistake. A child is dead! That's not something you forget in a hurry. People will be analysing this for years. And you know what they'll say?"

"What will they say, Mathew?"

"It all happened on my fucking watch!"

This man wasn't bullshitting, thought Grant. The Chief really was upset. Not so much for the dead kid, more for himself. Which was no more than he expected. But Grant couldn't have cared less.

"Think you're going to blow a gasket, Chief. Calm the fuck down. I couldn't control how he was going to do it. But he did what he did. He must have thought that was his only way in. He had inside information. And it was his call."

"Inside information? What does that mean?"

"He knew about the police stopping at the house for routine check-ups. He improvised. He used the situation to his advantage."

"What do you mean 'inside information'?"

Grant lowered his voice to a dry whisper. "It means that you're not the only fucking rat on the take."

A silence followed. Grant felt like laughing out loud when he thought of Chief Constable Smith digesting this new revelation.

Smith spoke at last, his voice weak, deflated. "I told you, when I gave you the Black dossier, that we were to be kept out of it. It was between you and Black. What's his name?"

"The name of my 'inside man'. You don't need to worry about him."

"But I do worry about him. He could compromise me. Does he know about our... relationship?"

"You mean, does he know I've been giving you bribe money

for the last twenty years? I don't think so. But you can rest easy, Chief. He's not going to cause you any trouble."

"Why is that?"

"Because he's dead."

A pause.

"And his name?"

"Detective Inspector Colin Patterson."

Another lengthy silence, except the sound of the chief constable's heavy, panicked breathing.

Grant continued. "He came to us, years ago. He came to *us*. No recruitment necessary. Been on the take for as long as I can remember. Arranged for the coppers to visit Black's house every afternoon. Told us all about it. Made sure no coppers were about when our man made his entrance. But the fucker got greedy. And you know greed is a sin. So, he's retired. Permanently."

"You've gone too far," said Smith, his voice faltering.

"Maybe. But I can go a lot further. Take a big step back, Mathew, and take a big breath with it. Do your fucking job and turn the other way. Just like you always do. Don't start getting all high and mighty. It's not worth it. You're in this up to your neck. So, embrace it, old friend, and enjoy all that money I've been paying you over all those long, long years. Pass my regards to the family."

He hung up.

"Everything okay, boss?" asked Nathan.

"Just another bent copper."

35

Castle Combe, Wiltshire. A hamlet sitting in the heart of the English countryside. A place plucked from a different time, unblemished by the horrors of modern architecture. Houses built from Cotswold stone the colour of honey, high-peaked roofs of split-stone tiles. Narrow streets and age-darkened taverns; a medieval church with a faceless clock; a humpbacked grey stone bridge spanning an ambling river. Chocolate-box England wrapped up in fairy-tale ribbons.

Black wasn't visiting for the scenery. He'd decided to drive down, a long journey from Glasgow to the south of England. But he didn't care. He needed space. He barely noticed the passing miles. He played music, played the radio, then switched it off, savouring the silence, and let his thoughts drift.

His wife and daughter were dead. Their existence on this planet snuffed out. A command had been issued, the deed was done. He needed to grieve. But while Peter Grant was alive, this was not a luxury Black allowed himself. A more immediate emotion bustled its way to the front of the queue.

Rage.

Pure and simple.

He had telephoned beforehand, to ask if he could visit. More than visit. Talk. They hadn't spoken for several years, but when Black heard his voice on the telephone, it was like no time had passed, their friendship an instant bond, spanning time and distance. Black had explained what had happened. From the freezing night on an Eaglesham road, to the cold bright afternoon his family were killed. About the man called Peter Grant. *Yes*, he'd said. *Come now.*

He arrived at a mid-terraced house overlooking Bybrook River. It was early evening, and cold, though not the brutal cold of Glasgow. Black had been driving for hours, but he wasn't tired. He parked the car, got his overnight bag, and made his way to the front door. Before he could knock, the door opened.

A man stood framed in the doorway. Small and wiry, clean-shaven, cropped grey hair, a lined, tanned face. Not tanned from the sun, but from the elements. A man who worked at his fitness. Penetrating blue eyes, deep set in a brow wrinkled with care. Dressed in dark pullover, blue jeans.

Major Kenny Devlin.

He gave a wide smile.

"Welcome, old friend."

They shook hands.

For the first time in days, Black felt a little of the weight in his heart lessen.

"Good to see you again, Major."

He followed the major into a small, comfortable living room. A log fire crackled. Like the exterior of the building, it was from a bygone age. Oak beam joists on the ceiling, thick stone walls painted plain white, shelves on one wall packed with rows of books, and in a corner on a rug, a bull mastiff lying sound asleep, stretched across several pairs of mountain boots. Two chairs, a wicker-topped coffee table. Heavy curtains keeping out any draughts. No television.

On the table were two glasses and a bottle of single malt Scotch whisky. Talisker.

"You hungry, Captain?"

"Thirsty." Black smiled.

Devlin poured himself and Black two large measures.

They clinked glasses.

"To the Regiment," said Devlin.

"To managing to stay alive," said Black.

"Thank God for small miracles. How did we manage that?"

"Christ knows."

"Perhaps he does."

They sat.

"He would make a fine watchdog, if he could stay awake," remarked Black.

Devlin chuckled. "Old Spud's earned the right to do bugger all. When you reach his grand age, you can let the world pass you by, and not give a damn."

"Is that what you're doing in the Cotswolds? Letting the world pass you by?"

"My wife, she liked it here. When she died, I never thought to leave. It's quiet. It's country life. A change from the army. Therapy for the soul, I think. Much needed after the experiences we've had."

Black nodded but did not say anything. He watched the whisky swirl in his glass.

"So," continued Devlin. "You're here. I'm glad you came. What are you going to do?"

"Ask for a top-up?"

Devlin filled his glass.

"Tell me, Major, what would you do?"

Devlin sat back and stared at the flames. "That's a question I knew you were going to ask. And I wonder why you're asking it."

Black gave a wry smile. "For advice."

"For permission. Or maybe absolution."

Devlin took a sip of his whisky and rested the glass on his lap. Spud the dog twitched its back leg, a low growl emanating from its chest.

"He's dreaming," said Devlin. "Dreaming about racing through the puddles, no doubt. When he was a younger dog. But like me, he's too old and too weary to do very much. You've come here seeking advice from an old man. Perhaps I'm not the best person to speak to."

"You're the only person I can speak to. You were the only person who could make sense of all the blood and guts. And I need to make sense of this."

"I was padre to the army for thirty years," said Devlin. "I was with the 22nd for ten of those years. And through all that, I'd never fired a bullet. Not even carried a gun. But when a young soldier came to me, questioning his actions after he'd just sent a bullet through another man's head, I told him that God forgives. And do you know why I said that?"

Black waited for the answer.

"Because I could. Because a padre is dispassionate. He cares, of course. He doesn't take sides. He doesn't judge. So, it was easy for me to dispense... what did I say earlier? Therapy for the soul."

"I understand that," said Black. "But when all the peripheral stuff is removed from the equation, when we're right down to the bare bones, and the only thing between a soldier and possible death is God, then suddenly God becomes important – the only thing in the whole universe that's important. So, what you say counts. At least in my book."

"Maybe. The 22nd Regiment saw the worst of it." Devlin

turned his head to look directly at Black. "But you were different, Adam."

Black cocked his head, quizzically. "How so?"

"You enjoyed it. Like no other man I've met."

Black took a deep breath, but found he wasn't disagreeing.

Devlin continued. "In a world where men are given guns and bayonets with the sole objective to kill the enemy, right and wrong becomes blurred. But there was still a line – a moral line – over which I tried to guide men not to cross. Unnecessary killing, revenge shooting. You know what I mean. I tried to be neutral, in a place where it was difficult for neutrality to exist."

"A conflict of morals," said Black quietly, more to himself. "That's why I'm here. You've seen what I've seen. The death, the killing. You've listened to the guilt. I can speak to you. What you say is important. My wife and daughter were murdered. What would you do, Major? You haven't answered my question. And it's the answer I need to hear."

Devlin didn't respond immediately. The fire sparked and crackled. Eventually he spoke.

"I've known you for fifteen years. I was with you in Afghanistan and Iraq. You've been through all manner of shit. But your training saw you through it. You have, how can I say, a skill. You ask me what I would do? Probably nothing. Pray, and look to God for answers. Find it in my heart to forgive. But that's me." He stood, and made his way over to Spud, and stroked his back. Then he turned to face Black.

"But you're asking the wrong question. If you were to ask me what I would do if I were you, I would say this – use your skills." Devlin fell silent.

Black waited. Suddenly his entire world focused in on the man who stood before him.

"You were trained to be a weapon," Devlin continued after a minute. "And by Christ, you were effective. So, to answer the question you should be asking – if I were you, if I were Adam Black, then I would let loose, and kill each and every bastard that had a hand in the murder of my family."

Black nodded.

His own sentiments exactly.

Black left early the next morning, a long drive ahead of him. He would stay with Fletcher and his family for a few more days, until the funeral. After that? Black would need space and solitude to implement his plans.

He did not have to say goodbye to the Major. He had gone out with Spud in the pre-dawn darkness, walking the country roads. He had left Black a simple note.

Godspeed, Captain.

Godspeed.

Black pondered on these words. There was no God. Only death.

And on that particular subject, Black was an expert.

36

The funeral followed four days later. The morning was bright. Sunlight dappled the trees; the wind was still; the air crisp. For this one moment, the world had paused.

The ceremony was simple, and private. Eaglesham Parish Church – an ancient, unassuming building. High white walls, grey tiled roof, joined to a steeple with a clock tower. Set halfway up a hill, overlooking the village park. Where Merryn had played, on the swings, on the roundabout, under the watchful eye of her mother. His wife. Where they had laughed and smiled and held hands. Their presence was everywhere. Their spirits suffused the grass, the trees, the air he breathed. They were all around, and inside him. In his mind, his heart, his soul.

A private ceremony. Family and close friends. The interior was small, intimate. Plain wooden rows of benches, varnished until they shone. Beside him, solemn, disbelieving; Jennifer's mother. Old and frail. But proud, fiercely independent, her husband having died years earlier, leaving her alone in a large rambling house in Thurso. She'd got the train down, booked into a hotel in Glasgow. Stoic, normally. Not today. Not this day.

Her fragile shoulders shook, as she fought the tears, but the tears came anyway.

There, his partner Simon Fletcher and his wife. Silent, faces pale and pinched. Heads bowed, as they listened to the quiet voice of the minister, who spoke with a gentle heartfelt sadness.

Others. Close friends. Black barely registered. Faces. Tears. A great cavernous sorrow.

Two white caskets. His wife and little daughter. Sleeping. *Dreaming what?* he wondered.

The caskets were carried to two hearses parked at the church entrance. The journey to the cemetery was short. A mile outside the village. A four-acre square, enclosed by high stone walls, surrounded by silver birch, pale and slender in the sun.

The caskets were placed by the grave, side by side, before being lowered. The small crowd of people looked on, silent. Numb. Black stepped forward, knelt down, placed a hand on each. A breeze whispered; trees stirred. The sun stayed constant.

Black closed his eyes, and let the tears come. Silent, desperate. The world was dead. His soul crushed. There was nothing. The colours had gone, and in their place, a canvas of darkness.

Black stood.

A reckoning was to be had. This was Black's new world.

Destruction.

Death.

Vengeance.

37

Despite the remonstrations of Fletcher and Adele, Black did not return to their house. Instead, that very evening, he booked into a hotel. He needed time on his own, he explained. To take stock. To grieve. He knew they needed their own space too. Nor could he return to work. Fletcher reassured Black there was no problem. Take as long as you want, he said. He and his small army of paralegals and secretaries would handle the caseload. No problem. Black guessed there would be plenty of problems, but was grateful. Plus, he was way past the stage of caring.

He booked into The Travellers Inn, on the road towards Glasgow Airport, paying cash up front for three weeks.

Fletcher went with him, and was dismissive of his choice of hotels. "This," he pronounced, "is a fucking shithole."

Black merely shrugged. It was clean, relatively inexpensive, and within easy reach of everything he might need. His house in Eaglesham was a place of death. If he had his way, he would demolish it, brick by brick, and then burn what was left.

The room was spartan, but functional. He unpacked a suitcase borrowed from Fletcher, and placed what few items of clothing he had in the single wardrobe and set of drawers. Anything else he needed, he would buy. He showered, changed, and went down to the restaurant for a quick meal. He returned to his room. He had to think.

He had to plan.

At his interview in the police station, an eternity ago, the cops had mentioned names. One name in particular. Tommy 'Teacup' Thomson.

It was a start. And Black had to start somewhere.

It was time.

Time to hunt.

38

Revenge killing. It will not be tolerated in the British Army. But it's the sweetest fucking dish you'll ever taste.

Observation by Staff Sergeant to new recruits of the 22nd Special Air Service Regiment.

Peter Grant was not a great believer in exotic holidays abroad.

Born in the east end of Glasgow in a squalid two-bedroomed tenement flat, the third son to a father who worked as a ship's welder, and who drank his earnings on weekends, and to a mother who accepted her husband's fists with a desperate resignation, young Peter Grant did not enjoy the best of upbringings.

He learned to keep a hold of any money he earned. And Grant earned money any way he could. He quickly absorbed himself into the gangland scene in Glasgow. By the age of sixteen, he was well known to the police for extortion. His ruthless and violent tendencies caught the attention of those higher up the food chain. They honed his skills. He was a quick learner. He stabbed his first man at seventeen. If someone needed to get a message, Peter Grant was sent. And Peter Grant liked to deliver. Scarring, maiming, torture. And killing, if required. It became clear he was psychotic. And someone with that tendency could climb quickly. But he was also clever. He saw opportunities, and took them. He saw the profits in drugs, and soon he and his two brothers had formed their own outfit – drugs, prostitution, racketeering, blackmail, bribery. He ruled by fear. And everyone, bar none, was afraid of Peter Grant.

His reputation grew. The tentacles of his empire spread, as far south as London, and then abroad. The years passed. His empire expanded. His two brothers died – one cancer, the other a gunshot in the chest. He was the only one left, the one in charge. The boss.

But the legacy of his youth remained with him. He had known hard times. He spent money on property, because that was a logical investment; on clothes, because he knew image was important. But not drink. Nor exotic holidays. That was simply a bridge too far, and his brain didn't compute such a luxury as something worthwhile.

When he went to Grand Cayman, accompanied by the ever-present Thor and Nathan, he didn't go to enjoy the sun, or the scuba, or fishing in the clear waters. It was purely business. Almost.

He was closing accounts. Laws were tightening, even there. This had to be done personally, before a notary. Huge sums of money were being transferred, and he wanted things tailed off. He had ten accounts, in ten different banks. In a few days' time, he would no longer require the services of offshore institutions.

They had arrived at Owen Roberts International Airport at mid-morning local time, booked into the Coral Reef Resort, and had lunch at Pelican Point overlooking the ocean, and then visited each of the banks he had accounts with, transferring funds, and then closing them for good.

The last bank was called Pacific Investment Holdings. An understated building in the centre of George Town, wedged amongst a cluster of expensive boutiques and restaurants, at the foot of the famous Seven Mile Beach.

Grant had an appointment with the manager, who was attentive and efficient.

"You're transferring the full amount, Mr Grant?"

"The full amount."

The bank manager nodded – whether the loss of his client's business had any impact was impossible to say. He remained impassive.

"Of course. So that will be four million, two hundred and eighty-five thousand dollars, after deduction of our closing expenses."

Fuckers, thought Grant. They all charged a closing fee, but this lot were sheer money-grabbing bastards – all in all, a one hundred and twenty-five-thousand-dollar charge for the privilege of closing the account. But also, it bought their silence. Getting information on customers from the Grand Cayman banks was like trying to rob Fort Knox with a penknife.

And Grant coveted his privacy when it came to finances.

"And which account are the funds going to?"

Grant had memorised the bank account details. He relayed the sorting code, account number and the name of the bank.

"And what is the name of the beneficiary."

Grant told him the name.

"And is there a reference?"

"Yes. Abacus."

The funds were transferred, electronically, all by the touch of a button, the account was closed, and the closing documents were signed by Grant, and witnessed by the bank's notary.

The entire transaction took less than thirty minutes.

Grant immediately made a phone call. The voice on the other end confirmed the money had been received.

"You have it all," he said.

The voice responded. "Yes."

"And Abacus is to your satisfaction?"

"Abacus is perfect."

"When can we complete?"

"One week. Routine paperwork. Legitimisation. That's what I like to call it."

"I like that word. Sounds sweet as a nut. Do it."

The three left the building. It was late afternoon. A short distance from them was the beginning of the coral sand of the Seven Mile Beach, regarded by many as the most beautiful beach in the Caribbean.

"You two can have the night off," said Grant. "Go and get drunk if you want. I'll meet you for breakfast tomorrow, nine sharp. We've got a plane to catch, so don't get too pissed."

"All the money's been transferred?" asked Nathan.

Grant nodded.

"What's happening? I'm in the dark, Uncle Peter. You need to tell me what's going down. I'm like... lost in all this secrecy."

"I need to tell you fuck all. But what I will say is that money sitting in a Grand Cayman Bank doesn't make us any profit. It just sits there. It sits there because it's proceeds of crime, and the cunts who run the banks here know it. So, they scoop up the interest, and charge million-dollar holding fees. You've heard the expression *Money makes money*? Well, that doesn't apply when it's tied up with these bastards. So it's being released. But the fewer people that know about it, the better for everybody."

Suddenly he wrapped his arms around his nephew and held him close.

"I love you," he whispered in his ear. "You'll know all about it soon enough." He kissed him on the cheek. "Now fuck off, both of you, and enjoy."

They separated, and Grant strolled along the promenade, admiring the sea glistening like a carpet of blue jewels under the sun. He made sure that when he travelled to Grand Cayman for his business transactions, he visited a very specific place. And it was important to Grant he was alone when he visited.

He made his way past beach bars and fish restaurants and wooden harbours. He enjoyed the feel of the warm sea breeze on his skin. He was wearing loose white casual trousers, a simple white T-shirt. He kicked off his sandals and felt the warm sand between his toes. It was the cleanest sand he had ever walked on. Thirty minutes later, his wanderings took him to a busy bar set a hundred yards back from the beach – The Blue Oyster. Little wooden tables were arranged outside, in an apparently random fashion, where people were eating and drinking and smoking. Men, mostly. Music from an old-fashioned jukebox wafted out, not loud. An old Elvis song.

Grant sat at a table. A young waiter served him.

"What can I get you sir?"

"What's on offer?"

The boy smiled. "Anything you want."

Grant smiled back. "Mineral water would be fine. Still. No ice."

The waiter nodded and swished away.

Grant relaxed and took the time to survey the men sitting at the other tables. One caught his eye. Mid-twenties, blond, medium-length hair, slim, olive skin. Exactly his type. Dressed in tight blue jeans, blue denim shirt. He noticed a small tattoo on the side of his neck. Grant felt an almost instant erection.

The man noticed Grant looking at him. He was with three others. He said something to them, left them, and made his way over to Grant.

"You look rather lonely." He smiled, showing a perfect row of white teeth.

"Very," replied Grant. "Join me."

"Would love to." He sat opposite Grant. The waiter returned with Grant's drink.

"Can I buy you anything?" asked Grant.

"Gin and tonic."

The waiter left.

"Can I buy anything else?"

The man looked at Grant archly. "I don't know. Maybe. It depends on how much you want to spend."

"How much can you take?"

The young man leaned closer, both elbows on the table, and looked directly into Grant's eyes. "I can take everything you have. Everything."

"Everything?"

"And for three hundred dollars, I can take a bit more."

"Three hundred dollars? That's a lot of money."

The young man leaned a little closer, his voice barely above a whisper. "And you can fuck me any which way you want. All night, if you want to."

Grant reached into his inside jacket pocket, pulled out his wallet, and put four hundred dollars on the table.

"A bit extra. For special attention."

The young man laughed, relaxing back in his chair. "You'll get it. Extra special. Whatever you want."

39

Teacup's reputation hinged on his ability to be easily located – if desperate people needed quick money, not caring about the thousand per cent interest rate, then Teacup was the loan shark they would look to. And many men and women did. Drug addicts, gamblers, alcoholics, prostitutes. People unable to get legitimate credit elsewhere and needed quick money to feed their kids. Teacup's business depended on the vulnerable, and he made plenty of profit from it.

But he could fix things too. Ex-boxer turned enforcer, a violent man. If people needed something done, then Teacup was the arranger. And Teacup rarely failed in coming up with the goods. He was a member of the Grant family and could fix most things. He could find the right drugs for the right people at four in the morning. He could supply clean young rent boys for High Court judges and prominent QCs any time, any place. And if money needed collecting, then Teacup enforced the Grant law. No payment meant broken kneecaps. Continued non-payment meant prolonged pain, and ultimately a brutal death. Teacup collected for Peter Grant, and whether it was simple extortion or blackmail of a high-profile politician, few failed to pay up. And those that didn't pay ended up disfigured or dead. Once you were indebted to Teacup, you were indebted for life.

If a person needed to find Tommy 'Teacup' Thomson, then that person would not have to look far.

But Teacup was no longer the man he used to be. He was out of hospital, had been for several weeks. But he still needed a stick to walk around. He had a pain in his hip, like a constant toothache. He got blinding headaches. Sometimes, if he bent down quickly, turned quickly, he got dizzy, his world spun. His jaw, fractured in two places, was sore when he chewed. Plus, and most importantly, his credibility had been tarnished. The so-called hard man of the Grant family had been put in hospital by one individual. Word spread quickly. His position in the chain of command had been affected. Once a close confidante of Peter Grant, now he was doing errands, on the street buying and selling drugs, slapping prostitutes back into line, collecting money. Crap jobs. Teacup was humiliated. And Peter Grant wanted him to feel it.

Teacup had been a bitter man all his life. Now he was bitter and disrespected. He woke every morning, and felt like shit. All because of one man.

It was a Wednesday afternoon. Teacup was leaving his bi-weekly session with the physio. Paid for by himself – this was his mess, so it was his problem. Such was the edict of Peter Grant. He got a call on his mobile. The man calling him was Nathan Grant.

The tone was clipped, all business. Any warmth had evaporated weeks back.

"There's a deal going down tonight."

"Okay. What's happening?"

"The old MOT station at Hillington. 2am. Polly King's got a bag of pure white for you."

"How much?"

"Fifty grand's worth. The money will be dropped off at your flat this evening."

"Sure. No problem. Nathan?"

"Yes, Teacup?"

Teacup paused, took a breath. The words came rattling out. He couldn't help himself.

"What the fuck am I supposed to do? I'm family. This guy, Adam Black. He was a fucking machine. I swear. It wasn't all down to me. He killed Blakely, who'd been paid a fortune to watch Damian. Don't squeeze me out." He took another breath. A word passed his lips which made his guts squirm. "Please."

A silence. Then Nathan spoke. "What do you want me to say, Teacup?"

"Speak to the man. Tell him..."

"Tell him what? Tell him his only son was killed in the street when you were supposed to be looking after him? No need to tell him that. He knows it already."

Nathan hung up.

Teacup swore. The man standing next to him opened the car door. His new chaperone. Ralph Lambert. Ex-wrestler. Barrel-chested; long muscular arms; wide neck. Head shaved to the bone. A tattoo of a skull on the back of each hand. Teacup was paying him three hundred pounds a day to be at his side. Clamped next to him, like a shadow. Low intellect, limited conversation. But Teacup didn't care.

Since Eaglesham, he'd lost more than his reputation.

He'd lost his nerve. All down to one man.

Adam fucking Black.

40

Finding Teacup was no major challenge to Black. His name was well known in certain parts. After asking a few discreet questions in pubs in the east end of Glasgow, Black was informed Teacup enjoyed the casino, and on any given night he could be found at the roulette wheel, or maybe the poker table.

Of the major casinos in Glasgow, the Albion was the biggest and grandest, designed in the manner of a mock-British colonial mansion, complete with slender white columns at the entrance, tall windows, dark wood floors. It consisted of three levels, the ground level full of traditional fruit machines and little booths with computer screens, for those who liked to try computerised gambling. The first level had exotically-named cocktail bars and two dance floors and a smattering of gaming machines. The top floor was the real thing. Roulette wheels; dice; blackjack; poker; craps.

Black sat himself in a corner, a tall glass of vodka and Coke at his table, which he did not drink. He watched. He had chosen a vantage point which allowed him to see all the tables, and people entering and leaving. The place got busy about eleven. It had a late liquor licence and was open all night. Plus, the drinks were cheap, which made sense, thought Black. Get the punters pissed, and they lose their caution. And when that's gone, the casino cleans up.

On the second evening of his surveillance, Teacup made an appearance. It was midnight. Black recognised him instantly. A muscular man, about five-ten, short brown hair, clean-shaven. Dressed in a discreet dark-blue suit, loose blue shirt opened at the collar. A boxer's face – heavy brows, broad, flat nose, lantern-jawed. When they last met on that freezing night on a road in Eaglesham over ten weeks ago, Black had broken several of his bones. Maybe caused some internal bleeding. Black noted he used a walking stick, his movements stiff. Too bad. Black watched him from a distance, his face veiled in shadow, fascinated by the figure who had attempted to kill him. Teacup spent a brief time on each of the gaming tables, sometimes winning, sometimes losing, until at last, settling down to a specific roulette wheel, spreading his chips about, perhaps randomly. Black would never know, nor did he care.

Teacup was accompanied by a man who spoke little, and who didn't gamble. Short and stocky, with a shaved bullet head, his neck wider than his face. Minder? Friend? Perhaps, after their little encounter in Eaglesham, Teacup felt the need for some protection.

Black remained at his table. Teacup stayed at the roulette wheel for over an hour. His friend went to the bar every so often and brought back drinks. At last, Teacup called it a night, scooped his chips up, and went to the cashier's booth to collect his money. Black never took his eyes off him.

They left together, Teacup and his friend. Black followed at a safe distance. Down the escalator to level one. Here, Teacup stopped to talk to someone. Then the next escalator to the ground floor. Black followed.

They got outside. It was cold. The pavement was adjacent to

a private car park for casino patrons only. The short, stocky man left. Teacup waited at the front door, talking into his mobile phone. Black lingered behind the main glass doors, able to see the back of Teacup's head.

A car pulled up. A black BMW X5 driven by Bullet Head. Teacup continued to talk for a few seconds, then got in. They drove off. Black jogged to his own car, parked close to the casino entrance, and followed.

They drove for half an hour to an industrial park on the outskirts of Glasgow, Black tailing at a discreet distance. The BMW parked outside an MOT station, the roller shutters closed, the lights out. It looked abandoned. Another car was already there, engine off, the silhouette of a driver visible. Black killed the headlights, and parked a hundred yards away. Teacup and Bullet Head got out. The other driver also got out, holding something. A white plastic bag. Teacup had a holdall slung over his shoulder.

Black decided it was time to move. He put on a tight-fitting pair of leather driving gloves, and opened the glove compartment. He pulled out a steel-handled claw hammer. He eased open his car door, shutting it gently, made his way towards them, hugging the shadows. There were no regular street lights. The only illumination was the occasional light on the wall of a building. He reached the BMW, crouching behind it. The men were in deep discussion. Black watched them for several seconds. He tightened his grip on the hammer. It was time.

Time to start a war.

He approached them, almost casually, emerging from the shadows, quiet as a wisp of smoke. The three men were unaware of his presence, until he was close up. They jerked round, startled.

"Evening."

He brought the hammer down, a thunderous blow, striking

Bullet Head hard on the area of bone between his eyes. He crumpled to the ground.

Teacup took a step back, shocked. "What the fuck!"

The third man sprinted back to his car, jumped in, and drove off, tyres screeching. Black let him. He was of no interest to him. Teacup stood motionless, trying to grasp what had happened. Black turned to face him.

"Remember me?"

Indecision rippled across Teacup's face. Black guessed what he was thinking – should he try to get back to his car? Should he fight? Should he do nothing and just wait to see what happened next?

Choices, choices.

"I don't want any trouble," said Teacup, the words tumbling out at frantic speed. He swallowed, thinking, then said, "You don't want to mess with me. You do that, and you mess with Peter Grant. You understand this?"

Suddenly, he swung his walking stick at Black, but the movement was weak, awkward. Teacup was still in recovery mode. Black had anticipated such a reaction. He stepped in and slammed his fist into Teacup's mouth. Teacup staggered back, dazed, landed on his backside. Black strode forward, kicked him in the groin. Teacup rolled over, scrunched up in pain.

Bullet Head stirred, moaning softly, trying to gain some movement in his arms and legs. He shifted over to his side, staring up at Black with glazed, unfocused eyes, and propped himself up on one elbow. He tried to speak, working his jaw, but the words were an incoherent mumble. Blood was flowing from his left eye. Black turned, regarded him with icy detachment, then brought the hammer down again, once, twice, three times. Bullet Head was silenced.

"You've fucking killed him!" croaked Teacup.

"Shame. But he deserved it. Anyone who associates

themselves with Peter Grant needs to understand they're going to die. Including you, Teacup."

"Please," said Teacup, between gasps. "I had no idea Damian was going to attack you that night. He was wild. Out of control. I was only there to look after him. It's the fucking truth. Things got out of hand. It should never have happened."

"Don't I know it."

Teacup had dropped his holdall. Black picked it up, and unzipped it. It was full of cash. Fifty-pound notes bundled together with elastic bands.

"Keep it," muttered Teacup. "There's fifty grand there. It's all yours."

"Thank you," said Black. "That's very generous."

"What are you going to do?"

"What do you think I'm going to do?"

"Please. We can be reasonable about this."

"Reasonable about what?"

Teacup licked his lips. "About this. Whatever the fuck this is. This situation."

Black stood over him, hammer in one hand. "That's exactly what this is, Teacup. A situation. You could say, when my wife and daughter were murdered in their own house, that was a situation too. Life is full of 'situations'. Until life ends."

"What are you going to do?"

Black bent closer. "Kill you. With this hammer. Just like your friend on the ground. You okay with that?"

"I had nothing to do with what happened to your wife and kid. These decisions were made way over my head. No way would I do something like that. I was never involved."

"You were involved from day one. Stand up."

With difficulty, Teacup got to his feet. He spat blood. "I've lost some teeth," he mumbled. His mouth was a mess. He looked at Black. He started to sob. "Please. Killing me won't get you any closer to Grant. He doesn't give a shit about me." Suddenly his face contorted into wild anger. "I hate the bastard. I hate him, and I hated his fucking son."

"But don't you get it, Teacup?" said Black, his tone almost reasonable.

"Get what?"

"This isn't about you."

"What?"

"This is about me. Killing you will make me feel a whole lot better."

"There's other ways of getting to Peter Grant. There's a deal going down. Fucking massive. Millions."

"And?"

"Please, if I tell you, then let me go. I'll forget all of this. You go your way, I go mine. Like nothing happened. And you can still get to Grant. What happened to your family was wrong. Plain fucking wrong. You want revenge. Who wouldn't? I get that."

"You get it?"

"Sure."

"You married, Teacup? You got kids?"

Teacup shook his head.

"So what do you get exactly? Tell me about this massive deal."

Teacup wavered on his feet. "I don't feel so good," he mumbled.

"Tell me."

"I don't know much." His breathing was laboured. "But he has an accountant who works for him, in some fucking office in Aberdeen. He helps to launder his money. His name is something like William... Willard Chapman, or Chapford. Stupid fucking name. He knows all about it. Get to him, and you can get to Peter Grant."

"Is that it?"

"What more do you want? I can't give you anything else, because I don't know anything. I'm just a fucking foot soldier."

Black nodded. "A foot soldier? Interesting expression. Fair enough. Tell you what, Teacup. You head back to the car, and I'll check up on this accountant. But if I find that you're lying..." Black pointed an admonitory finger at him.

"No way." Teacup took a tentative step back, then turned to start a shambling half-run for the black BMW only twelve feet away.

Black took four long strides forward and locked his arm around Teacup's neck.

"Really?" he hissed in his ear. "As simple as that? You knew there was only one way."

Teacup struggled, clawing at Black's arm, but he was weakened, his effort to dislodge Black feeble.

"My family were shot and killed," said Black. "So you pay the price, my friend."

Black squeezed. Teacup gasped, squirmed, kicked out. His movements lessened; seconds passed. He hung limp. Black continued to squeeze, then released. Teacup's dead body slumped to the ground. Black struck his head several times with the hammer, to make sure. One thing he'd learned with the SAS – no half measures. When you mean to kill, then kill.

A drug deal gone wrong, he thought. That's how it will appear, at first glance. Two dead villains. He placed the hammer in the lifeless hand of Tommy 'Teacup' Thomson, ex-boxer, ex-hardman, ex-everything.

Black retrieved the holdall, and returned to his car.

Next stop – the accountant.

41

Peter Grant did not hear about Teacup's demise until the day after the occurrence. It was yet another meeting Nathan was dreading. Teacup was a cousin, albeit distant, and therefore family, though well down the pecking order. He'd slipped further for failing to prevent Damian's death. Ostracised, virtually. Grant still used him for a certain street slyness and occasional brutality when required. Days could go by before they might talk, and even then, any instructions were usually given by an intermediary such as Nathan, or someone else close. But Teacup was still family, invited to all family gatherings – birthdays, christenings, weddings, funerals.

Nathan found Grant at the Ten Bells Boxing Club, where he trained twice a week. A large brick-built ex-council property, formerly used for archiving and records. He'd bribed some officials, bought it at discount, stripped it out, installed a full-sized boxing ring, had gym equipment put in, heavy-duty leather punchbags, speed balls, free-standing bags, had showers built, and changing rooms. Grant made it a habit of remembering his roots, and liked people to know he did. The club was on a street not far from the Barras Market, in the east end of Glasgow, near where he had lived as a boy. Kids under twelve and the unemployed could train for free. Compliments of Peter Grant. If a local boy showed some talent, Grant would take him under his wing, arrange fights, get him managed. Grant liked to be regarded as a benefactor, a good Samaritan, a pillar of the community. But discreet drug deals went on at the Ten Bells, another small part of the Peter Grant crime factory.

Nathan gave him the news. As ever, he seemed to be the bearer of bad tidings. Grant was ending a third round of sparring, complete with headgear and gumshield. Nathan stood to one side, watching his uncle with a mixture of admiration and dread. The man was over sixty-five but moved in the ring like a thirty-year-old. He was agile and strong, and fit as any athlete. He punched hard and accurate like a professional.

The bell sounded. Grant pulled off his headguard, stepped through the ropes, and jumped down beside Nathan.

"Here comes fucking bad news," said Grant, half-jokingly. "Here, help me with these."

He lifted his gloves. Nathan untied the laces.

"So, what are you so glum-faced about?"

"I'd rather talk in private."

"Let me have a shower first."

"It can't wait."

Grant raised an eyebrow.

"Must be serious."

"It is."

Nathan pulled off the boxing gloves. Grant took a deep swig from a plastic bottle containing an energy drink, then made his way to a partitioned-off room which was used as an office of sorts. A couple of men were sitting at a table, drinking tea. Grant told them to leave, which they duly did.

"Do I need to sit down," asked Grant, a hint of humour still in his voice.

Nathan shrugged. "It's up to you, Uncle Peter." He took a deep breath. "Bad news. Shit news, actually."

Grant waited.

"Teacup's dead."

Grant fixed Nathan a long stare.

"Are you fucking kidding me?"

Nathan could only shake his head.

"What happened?"

"He was doing a deal. Buying gear. At the location something went wrong. Teacup and Ralph were killed."

"And who the fuck is Ralph?"

"Just a guy. Professional wrestler. Teacup hired him to watch his back since... you know what."

"Since I know what? You're speaking in riddles. Since when does Teacup need a fucking bodyguard, when my name's the only protection he needs. What anyone needs."

Nathan licked his lips, as he formulated his response. "Since the night Black put him in hospital."

"The night Damian was killed, you mean," said Grant. "Just say it. Who was selling the drugs?"

"Polly King."

Grant nodded. "That fucking heroin junky piece of slime. If he was doing the drop, there's no way he did this. The guy's a spineless shitbag. How much are we talking about?"

"We lost fifty grand. My theory is, Polly took a chance, kept the money and the drugs. Now he's hiding."

"Too fucking right he's hiding. Wake up, Nathan. No way Polly took out two guys. He couldn't take out his fucking granny. If we find Polly, we find out who did this. Get word out that he's not in trouble. Reel him in and get him talking."

"If he didn't do it, then who would dare?"

Grant wiped a sheen of sweat from his forehead. "Someone with one major axe to grind. Someone who can take out two men. Who would dare? Good choice of words. Who dares wins. Any thoughts?"

Nathan did not reply. He knew the question did not require an answer. He knew the answer all along, but didn't want to believe it. Only one man fitted the bill. Captain Adam Black. The gnawing doubts he had harboured since the involvement of Joshua, were blossoming into something new and fresh.

Fear.

42

The accountancy firm of Chadwick and Co. was difficult to find. An office above a charity shop situated in the north of Aberdeen. A backstreet establishment, a hundred yards from the main thoroughfare, down a couple of side streets, in an area comprising vacant 'to let' units, charity outlets and bookmakers. Black imagined the place to have been bustling before the price of oil slumped, populated by little bijou coffee shops and bistros. A ten-minute walk to St Machar's Cathedral, a twenty-five-minute stroll to Union Street, the heart of Aberdeen. But when oil reached an all-time low, and Aberdeen was dragged down with the rest of the country in post credit crunch, suddenly rentals weren't being paid, staff were laid off, loans were defaulted. Professionals, such as accountants, found it just as tough as anyone to turn a buck. And so some delved down a darker route.

The man who owned the firm of Chadwick and Co. was called Willard Chadwick. Close enough to the name given by Teacup in his dying moments for Black to rationalise it was probably the same individual. Chadwick was a big barrel-chested man about sixty; florid complexion, heavy jowls. He had a full head of thick hair, dyed unnaturally black. He wore a three-piece suit, a size too small, the buttons on his waistcoat bulging. Once, a long time ago, he may have been described as athletic. A rugby player perhaps, thought Black. But too many pints, too much whisky and fine meals, and too long sitting on his arse, had eradicated any semblance of former glory. Chadwick was a man trying pathetically to cling to the vestiges of another era.

Black had phoned the office, to be answered by a surly-voiced female. He wanted an appointment with Mr Chadwick. Black was told he was busy, and that he should call back. Black was dogged. He wanted an appointment as soon as possible. Otherwise he would seek advice elsewhere as to how he could invest two million pounds. He was asked for his number. Within two minutes, Willard Chadwick himself telephoned back, and suggested they meet in his office. He was flexible. That afternoon was arranged.

Chadwick and Co. comprised little more than a reception area, an office and a toilet. The décor was uninspiring. Chadwick's office itself was surprisingly spacious, with little in it except a couple of filing cabinets, a desk and some chairs. The paint was faded, the carpet thin and needing a clean.

Black sat on one side of the desk. Opposite sat Chadwick, meaty elbows resting on the tabletop. The air was heavy with the scent of his aftershave. The single window behind him offered a view of the opposite building.

"Thank you for seeing me at such short notice," said Black.

"Not at all, Mr Black. My pleasure. I'm always interested in a man who wants to invest." Chadwick spoke in a deep baritone, almost musical. A singer, in his day.

"You're highly recommended."

"That's always good to hear. Another of my clients?"

"You could say that. He said you were discreet. Are you a discreet man, Mr Chadwick?"

"Naturally. When it comes to a large amount of funds – two million sterling I think you said? – then discretion is paramount. Crucial, I would say."

"It's a lot of money. It needs a safe pair of hands."

"Absolutely," replied Chadwick, flashing bright white teeth. "Where is the money now, Mr Black?"

"Here's the thing. It's in a large suitcase in my hotel bedroom."

The smile on Chadwick's face drooped. Black was reminded of a sad clown.

"You mean it's cash?"

"Hard cash."

Chadwick immediately stood, his bulk blocking out the daylight. "I'm sorry, Mr Black," he said, his tone dismissive. "I can't help you under any circumstances. I can't handle cash of that amount. Anti-money laundering, you understand. This is a reputable firm. I would suggest you look elsewhere for financial advice."

Black nodded and stood as well. "Of course. I understand perfectly. Sorry to have troubled you."

He left the building, and meandered his way into Aberdeen centre, to Union Street. It was three thirty in the afternoon, the weather drab and dreary, the streets not particularly busy. He stopped at one of the many coffee shops, and ordered a double-shot black coffee. He sat at the window, watching people pass by. He was in no hurry. He took out his wallet and pulled out a small photograph of Jennifer and Merryn, both smiling, both eating ice-cream cones, wearing red woolly hats, their cheeks flushed with the cold. He could not remember exactly when the picture had been taken.

He took a deep shuddering breath. Every waking moment

was a struggle to keep his emotions in check. He had learned many lessons in the army, especially the Special Services. Focus. Harness your feelings. Use them. Anger, hatred, even sadness. They were all positive, if managed properly. Especially anger. The regiment expected a cool head in battle. Detachment. But at the critical moment, at the point of killing, uncork the emotions for as long as required. Controlled aggression. Then rein them back in and move on. There were some who thought that soldiers in the SAS were borderline psychotic. Black reflected that there was probably some truth in this. Right now, he was in kill mode. Emotions bubbling under a paper-thin veneer. And when the moment finally came, when he could confront Peter Grant, for that brief time, all hell would break loose.

The mobile phone in his inside coat pocket buzzed, as he had expected. Sooner than he thought.

"Yes."

"Mr Black?" It was the voice of Willard Chadwick. "We should meet."

"Yes."

"Duthie Park. There's a blue bench beside the bandstand. I'll see you there at five fifteen this afternoon."

"Sounds good."

Chadwick hung up. Black put the photograph of his family back in his wallet and sipped his coffee. He had time to kill.

43

"You're a hard man to find."

The man who sat opposite Peter Grant was thin, spindle-shanked, emaciated almost, dressed in an oversized sheepskin jacket that looked like a throwback to the seventies. Sunken cheeks, grey complexion, a twisted beak of a nose. There was a pint of lager on the table in front of him, and a packet of cigarettes. Polly King. Drug dealer and pimp. He looked ill, as if he hadn't slept for a week. He was agitated. His eyes darted about like small black fireflies. He lifted the pint glass to his mouth and gulped down some lager. The tremble in his hand was plain to see.

"Relax," soothed Grant. "We don't have a problem here."

Polly King had finally been located in a squalid one-bedroomed flat rented by one of his prostitutes, in a town seven miles from Glasgow, called East Kilbride. Grant had put it out that he was looking for Polly, and anyone who helped collected five hundred pounds.

It was easy money, and the prostitute talked. Nathan and three others picked him up and escorted him to a quiet pub in the south side of Glasgow, on Victoria Road, and one which

Grant owned. Grant was waiting for him. He wanted to hear this first hand.

"Sorry to disagree," replied Polly. "But from where I'm sitting there's one huge fucking problem."

"Calm down, Polly. I'm only looking for some clarification. You know what I'm talking about."

Polly's eyes flickered from Grant to the packet of cigarettes. "Can I go outside and have one first?"

"You can have one right here."

"Is that allowed?"

Grant laughed, though there was a metallic undertone. "I own this establishment. And what I say goes. So, if you want to destroy your lungs, then be my guest. It's a disgusting habit, Polly."

Polly nodded, took a cigarette from the packet, a lighter from his jacket pocket, and lit up.

"Okay," continued Grant. "You know why you're here. It seems over the last few days, you've been evading me. That's the way it looks. I'm sure that's not right. Is it?"

"No, never, Mr Grant."

Grant gave a cold smile. "Did you kill Teacup?" he asked quietly.

Polly took another hefty gulp of lager, and when he eventually spoke, his eyelids flickered like the wings of a fly. "I didn't touch anyone, I swear. The whole fucking thing was mad." He took another deep drag.

"I believe you. My nephew thinks otherwise. He thinks you saw an opportunity. He thinks that you killed Teacup and his friend, so you could take the money and keep the drugs. You could sell the drugs on again, and flip them over for another fifty grand. That's a lot of money. Life-changing, for some. Isn't that right, Nathan?"

Nathan, sitting beside Grant, opposite Polly, nodded. "That's how I see it. The only logical explanation."

Polly's eyes shifted from Nathan to Grant. "Are you kidding? No way would I do that. I know it looks bad. But I never got one penny of that money. I'm a businessman, Mr Grant. Teacup and I had an arrangement. I sell, he buys. I hid because, well, I was scared shitless."

"What were you scared of?" asked Grant.

"You! I thought you'd planned it. I thought you were trying to squeeze me out."

Grant nodded slowly. He was beginning to lose patience. But this meeting had to be played cool.

"You thought I would kill both you and Teacup? You know I wouldn't do that. Not to family. Plus – it wouldn't make any... economic sense. You're a reliable source. We get on well because we have common interests, and those interests make us both money. I'm simply trying to get to the bottom of what happened. What did happen, Polly?"

Another deep inhalation.

"It was crazy. A nightmare. We met at the MOT place at Hillington. Where we normally meet. I got out of my car. I had the gear in a bag. Teacup and another guy were out of their car, and Teacup was carrying a sort of holdall. Probably had the cash in it. We were talking. Just talking. You know Teacup. He was never really one for the small talk. But I like to chat. I guess it's nervous energy. So, I was asking how things were, and how he was keeping. Being sociable. I knew he'd been in hospital. Suddenly, out of nowhere, a big fucker appears. Dressed in a suit. The light wasn't great. I never got a good look at his face. He was carrying a hammer. He just walked up, like he was strolling in a fucking park, and cracked Teacup's pal on the head. The blood was gushing everywhere. Like a fountain. Teacup's pal dropped like a fucking stone."

Polly took another gulp of lager. Grant clenched his teeth in exasperation but contained his anger. Just.

Polly continued. "I've never seen anything like it, I swear. He just dropped right down. The first thing I knew I had to do was get the fuck right out of there. You get that, Mr Grant? So, I ran. Straight back to my car and got away."

"He didn't chase you?"

"That's the funny thing. He didn't seem to give a shit about me. He let me go."

"Can you describe him?" It was Nathan who asked the question.

"The light was bad you understand. But he was a big guy. Over six feet. As I said, dressed smartly. Dark hair. He didn't try to hide his face or anything. He wasn't wearing a hoodie or a balaclava. It's like he didn't care that I saw him."

"Didn't care," repeated Grant softly.

"He just walked up," said Polly. "That was what was so fucking sinister about the guy. It was almost casual. He wasn't in a rush. It was like he enjoyed it. What he did was like routine. I tell you, Mr Grant, he was one scary fucker."

"I get the picture, Polly. I can be a scary fucker too."

"Of course." He reached over for another cigarette.

"That's enough, Polly," said Grant. "I can tolerate one of those fucking cancer sticks. But you're pushing it now."

Polly accepted this with an obsequious nod. "Absolutely." He fidgeted, blinked. "And the gear? I've still got it. And seeing as I never got paid. Maybe we can still do a deal. Business is business, after all."

"Business is business," said Grant. "What were you selling?"

"Pure white. Three kilograms."

Grant knew his drugs, as had Teacup. The street value of heroin was about a hundred thousand per kilo, for quality stuff. Even with the loss of fifty grand, there was still a sizeable profit.

And Polly was a valuable source in the narcotics industry. Business is business, thought Grant. The wheels of industry still had to turn.

"Set it up, Nathan. We'll arrange something tonight. Fifty thousand for three kilos. Now fuck off back to the shithole where we found you."

Polly stood, finished off his pint, and said, "Thank you, Mr Grant. A pleasure."

When Polly had left the premises, Grant turned to Nathan.

"I've been slack. I should have finished Black off with his wife and brat."

"If it was Black."

"It was Black all right. Time to pay him a visit. I need him dead."

"But we don't know where he is," argued Nathan. "He's not at work. He's not gone back to his house. He could have left the country for all we know."

"But I do know," replied Grant. "Or at least will know. One phone call, and I can find him. I think it's about time Thor was usefully employed."

44

Duthie Park. About forty acres of parkland edging on the banks of the River Dee. Black had never been to the place, but he located the bandstand without difficulty. And sure enough, there was the shiny blue park bench. It was 5.05pm. Black strolled over, as if he hadn't a care in the world, and sat. It was freezing cold. He wore a herringbone Crombie coat, gloves, scarf, but the cold still bit deep. He thought back to the woollen hat his wife had given to him that night in Eaglesham, and suddenly wished he'd kept it and was wearing it now. He took a long deep breath, fighting a strong impulse to stand up and berate the cruelty of life. Fat lot of good that would do him. He'd bought a cup of coffee to take away and sipped it while he waited.

The place was deserted save a couple of young kids playing on a monkey puzzle fifty yards distant, being watched by a woman sitting on a wooden bench.

Two men approached, walking nonchalantly along a path towards him. One was Willard Chadwick. The other he did not recognise. He was big, as tall as Chadwick, but twenty years younger, wearing an understated dark suit and tie, a grey overcoat. Spare of physique. His hair was cropped a half inch from his head. He walked with an easy, almost athletic economy of movement. A man of lethal capabilities. Ex-military? Perhaps.

"Do you mind if we join you, Mr Black?" said Chadwick. "Let me introduce you to my associate, Mr Kowalski."

Kowalski gave the briefest of nods. "Pleasure to meet you, Mr Black." He remained unsmiling. He did not offer a handshake, and neither did Black.

"Kowalski? Polish?"

"My father was from Chorzów. We moved to Britain when I was very young."

"Chorzów. Down in the southern regions, if I recall," said Black.

"I'm impressed, Mr Black. You've visited Poland?"

"Amongst other places."

Chadwick sat beside him. Kowalski remained standing.

"That was an interesting chat we had," said Chadwick.

"Really? I got the distinct impression you found the whole thing offensive."

Chadwick laughed quietly, with little trace of humour. "We talked about being discreet. One has to be discreet about certain things. You came to me with a proposition, and it might be that we are interested in helping you."

"We?"

"Myself, obviously, Mr Kowalski and another man, who you may meet presently, should matters come to fruition. Would you still like us to try to help you?"

"Very possibly. Depending on the conditions, naturally."

"Naturally. But given the sensitive nature of our discussions, would you mind if Mr Kowalski took certain precautions?"

"I'm not sure I follow."

"We need to be sure no one else is listening in to our little chats," said Kowalski. He spoke perfect English, no trace of an accent. "Privacy and discretion. Important words in our profession."

"I understand. Very wise."

Black stood, while Kowalski patted him down, searching for wires and devices.

Kowalski nodded to Chadwick. Black sat down.

"One can never be too careful," said Chadwick, his voice like silk. "So, to resume. You have two million to invest. I think that's what you said."

"Correct. To be easily accessed when and where I want it."

"And I assume the cash is savings accumulated over many, many years of hard work and thrift." Chadwick grinned.

"That, coupled with a deep aversion of our banking system." Black grinned back.

"Quite right," agreed Chadwick. "You'll not be the first to distrust the banks. And who can blame you, especially in this uncertain climate we live in. Where is the money at this moment?"

"In my hotel room."

"Not the safest place to keep it."

"As safe as I can think of, right now."

"How did you get my name, Mr Black?"

"Someone I know said you were reliable for this sort of thing. A colleague of mine. Someone who would prefer I didn't mention their name. Like you, he covets his privacy."

Chadwick nodded, cheeks rosy in the cold. "Of course. No names. Still, a reference is useful. After all, we've never met you before. We have to be careful who we do business with."

"If you need a name," said Black, "how about Pound Sterling. That usually removes any doubts."

He slowly placed his hand in his inside coat pocket, and drew out a plain brown envelope.

"There's fifteen thousand pounds here. For you. Call it a gift.

To show that I have money, and that I'm serious. Take it. If you're still not happy, then keep it. And I'll take my business elsewhere."

Chadwick took a deep breath, darted a side glance at Kowalski, who gave a slight twitch of his shoulders. Black read the signs. These men didn't give a damn about anything except the money. They were greedy, and blind, and saw an opportunity.

"I think we can help you here." Chadwick took the envelope, and tucked it in his pocket. "But you understand, the risks are high. We would need to see all the money, to ensure that this is real, that you're a serious investor. We would be seeking a down payment of one hundred thousand pounds, for initial overheads, and a fifteen per cent cut of the gross amount."

Black pursed his lips. "That's pretty steep commission."

"As I said, the risks are high. We will not negotiate on this. If you don't want to deal with us, then we have no problem, and you can go your way and live out your suitcase for the next few years, and someone else can launder your hard-earned savings. And we'll see how far you get."

Black sighed. "I don't really have a choice. So, what now."

"We can meet tonight. Bring the money with you. Have you heard of a town called Macduff? It's forty miles north from here. I have a flat there. A bolthole, you might say. But it's safe, and quiet, and we won't be disturbed. If you want to go ahead with this, then we'll meet you there at nine o'clock. It's on the river front, and the view is spectacular. Bring your suitcase, Mr Black."

Black looked at him, askance. "You want me to bring all of it? That seems a little risky to me. You could end up keeping it and throwing me away for fish bait."

Chadwick gave a brittle smile. "You said you had two million.

Two million it is. We're not going to undertake this venture for any less. The risks are extreme. You'll have to trust us, Mr Black."

"It seems all rather one-sided – I give you the money, and you keep it. What will you do with it? Where does it go? I need some assurance."

"We'll give you the specifics tonight. Needless to say, it's invested in offshore accounts, in safe havens. Places where certain authorities can't look. It's complex. Beyond that, there are no assurances. It's the game you're in. You need your money laundered, and we're offering to help. You came to us. That's the best you're going to get. Take it or leave, Mr Black."

"Fair enough."

Chadwick wrote the address in Macduff on a piece of paper, and gave it to Black. They stood, and shook hands.

"Tonight, at nine. We'll see you there."

"Looking forward to it, gentlemen."

Chadwick and the man called Kowalski left.

Black watched them go. The night would be interesting. The quiet town of Macduff was soon to bear witness to a little carnage.

Death was coming to supper.

45

G rant knew who to contact. The conversation was brief.
"You have everything you need?"

The voice on the other end of the line spoke in staccato-like bursts.

"You have all the funds," said Grant. "Abacus is one hundred per cent rock solid. We can get this over the line. Let's say in three days?"

The voice responded.

"Good," continued Grant. "We've fucked about long enough. And one other thing. Where can I find Adam Black?"

A pause. Then the voice spoke.

Grant hung up.

Sitting at the door of the conservatory was the massive bulk of Thor, slab-like hands resting on his lap, arms wider than a man's thigh, bull neck.

"I've got a job for you," said Grant. "One you might enjoy."

46

B lack drove the forty miles from Aberdeen to Macduff and got there an hour early. He made sure to drive by the flat Chadwick claimed he owned, slowing down. It was on the first floor of an impressive tenement of blond sandblasted stone with fresh white framed windows, and shiny black balustrades lining the stairs to the front entrance. It looked directly onto the harbour front, where blue and red fishing boats were moored, bumping and swaying on the choppy waters of the River Deveron. Chadwick was right. Looking out the front window, the view would be stunning.

Black wasn't there for the view.

Macduff was set on a steep hill. Black made sure to park a discreet distance from the rendezvous, not too close, on a side street where no one would notice him. He sat waiting. At quarter to nine he made his way there, carrying a large sports bag strapped over his shoulder.

The entrance was a locked communal door with press-button intercom system. Black pressed 1/1. A moment passed, then the line crackled, and the voice of Chadwick responded.

"Yes?"

"It's Black."

The door suddenly buzzed, the lock clicked open, and Black entered.

The stairs were grey stone with plain wooden banisters, the walls painted dark green, illuminated by flush mounted sconces, providing a muted amber glow. Drab, but clean. No graffiti, no rubbish piled up. Black got to the first floor. Chadwick was waiting. He had changed from his suit, and wearing casual and flamboyant clothing – blue flannels, open-necked green shirt, white sports jacket. The air around him was suffused with a heady mix of aftershave and whisky. His eyes gleamed when he spied the sports bag.

"I'm so glad you came," he said. "Please do come in to my humble abode." His voice boomed when he spoke.

He beckoned Black in, smiling a fantastic white smile.

Black entered a hallway, thick red carpet, white walls adorned with numerous small oil paintings of landscapes and cottages, and other forgettable images.

"The door on the left," said Chadwick.

He emerged into a living room, of regular dimensions, with furniture Black would have described as slightly dated. A fawn-coloured suede couch with lime-green cushions, two heavy black leather chairs, a television in one corner, a drinks cabinet in another, an oval-shaped coffee table in the centre, same red carpet. On the walls, scattered about like pimples on a white skin, were more small oil paintings. The far side comprised bay windows, scarlet velvet curtains, closed, shutting out the street lights.

Standing by the chairs were two men. One was Kowalski, wearing the same suit from earlier. Another man stood two feet from him. He was six inches shorter but built like a small tank. He was casually dressed, wearing a plain, faded, green T-shirt, blue jeans, heavy brown boots. Mountain boots, so Black noted, possibly with steel toecaps. His upper arms bulged with muscle, his neck thick and corded. Head shaved, features pinched in a round flat face.

Chadwick maintained a constant smile throughout.

"Mr Black, this is Mr Holomek." The man nodded at Black, expressionless.

"Let me guess. Polish?"

The man spoke with a heavy accent. "Romanian."

"I see."

"Now, Mr Black," continued Chadwick, "there are certain formalities which must be adhered to, if you don't mind. For everyone's protection. Could you put the bag on the floor, please."

"Of course." Black placed the holdall between his feet.

Kowalski stepped forward, and frisked him, expertly.

"We have to be certain you didn't come with any sinister intent, you understand," said Chadwick.

"You mean have I brought any guns or knives. Please, Mr Chadwick, we're here to do business. We're not here to kill each other."

"Of course not." Chadwick laughed, though to Black, it rang with a tinny overtone.

Kowalski produced a small black rectangular object, about the size and shape of a TV remote control. He pressed a button, and it emitted a low-pitched whine.

"We have to be sure there's no eavesdroppers," said Chadwick. "One cannot be too careful. Especially where money's concerned."

"Money," replied Black. "It can change people."

"For the better, I hope," said Chadwick.

Kowalski swept it slowly around Black's body, from neck down to shoes, then hovered it over his holdall.

"He's clean."

Chadwick's smile broadened further. "There we are. Now we can get down to business. A drink, Mr Black?"

"Whisky would be nice, if you have any. Neat."

"A man after my own heart. Any preference? I have a wide selection."

"You choose. If it's wet, I'll like it. Though I'm partial to a Glenfiddich."

"Excellent choice." Chadwick went over to the drinks cabinet, and fixed Black a whisky in a crystal glass. Meanwhile, Kowalski and Holomek kept their attention fixed on him, in a manner many would have found unnerving. Black had encountered such men many times. Dangerous men. Men well versed in routine killing and who were good at it. Black's senses were heightened, poised for the slightest movement, a glance, a seemingly innocent shrug, anything which could spell danger.

Chadwick handed him the glass. "Please, have a seat. Let's get comfortable."

Black sat at one end of the couch, the hand he was using to hold the glass, placed on the armrest. Kowalski sat on the other side of the couch, Chadwick and Holomek each taking the leather chairs opposite.

"You've brought the money, I see," said Chadwick.

"I have. As you instructed. I'm interested in what you intend to do with it."

"So you should be," said Kowalski, taking up the conversation, assuming an easy smile. He was sitting at an angle, facing Black as he spoke. He kept one hand under his jacket, as if resting it in his inside pocket. "Essentially it requires to be laundered." He spoke in a soft, clear voice, each word perfectly enunciated. "This is what you are asking us to do. And as you will know, laundering money which forms proceeds of crime, is now a high-end risky business."

Black sipped his whisky. "High risk, high fees. You're going to get exceptionally well paid for your services."

"It's the nature of the business we're in. It's a complex matter. We need the cooperation of certain banks and financial intermediaries. We have networks at our disposal which ease the flow, shall we say. But everyone needs their cut, otherwise the network breaks down."

"Of course," said Black. Bullshit. But he had to keep the game going. "Okay. So, I give you my hard-earned two million. Do I get any assurances at all? You take my money, and I never see you again. It seems to me that this high-end risk you talk about is all at my end."

"As I've already explained, Mr Black," blustered Chadwick. "It's all about trust. Remember, it was you who came to us."

Black pursed his lips, as if debating inwardly. "It seems just a little too... easy, handing over the lot. Once it's gone, it's gone. Perhaps we could start with a smaller amount. If what you do impresses me, then we can start talking about trust."

"We don't work on that basis," said Kowalski. "We don't undertake this type of work for *smaller amounts*. You mentioned the figure of two million, and that's the figure we'll take the risk for. And you've brought the money with you, so it must have been your intention to invest it with us."

"Invest? Is that what you do with it? Where do you invest it?"

"Certain banks. Brokers. Property developers. Corporations. Businesses which take cash."

"That's not very specific. I was expecting details. Maybe we should rethink."

The Romanian stirred. "Let's stop fucking about." His accent was heavy and jarring, a contrast to his colleague. "Give us the fucking money. Right now."

Black appraised him for five seconds, bewilderment on his face. "Excuse me?"

"I said – *give us the fucking money.*"

A silence followed. Another five seconds. Holomek fixed Black a leaden stare.

"Fuck it!" shouted Chadwick suddenly. His smile had gone. His face now appeared drawn, haggard, mouth set. All traces of bonhomie vanished. "It wasn't supposed to happen like this." He shot a venomous glance at Holomek, then appraised Black. "Sorry for my friend's abrasiveness. You were supposed to hand us the money, and we part company in a civilised manner, and that would be the end of it. That was the plan."

Black stared at Chadwick, his expression a mixture of bemusement and indignation. "Plan?"

"I'm afraid Mr Chadwick has a misguided view on how this works," broke in Kowalski. His voice took on a metallic undertone. "My friend, Mr Holomek, however, is a plain speaker. He has made our position clear. The truth is, we need your money. But we don't need you." He produced a pistol from his inside jacket, possibly from a holster strapped under his arm. It was small, a .38 compact revolver. At close range, it was still powerful enough to knock a hole through a man's chest.

Black gave a short harsh laugh. "You're fucking idiots."

"I'm the one holding the gun," said Kowalski, his voice measured, reasonable. "And you're the one about to give us all your money and then die with a bullet in your brain. Who's the fucking idiot."

"Before you pulled the gun, you should at least have checked what was in the holdall. You're in for an unpleasant surprise, gentlemen."

"Kill him," said Holomek, voice like gravel.

"Please!" cried Chadwick. "You promised it wouldn't be here!"

"Check the bag," said Kowalski.

Holomek stood, skirted round the coffee table, and picked

up the holdall still sitting at Black's feet. All the while Kowalski kept the pistol trained on him.

Holomek returned to his seat, placing the bag on his lap. He unzipped it. He pulled out a single roll of twenty-pound notes, bound up in an elastic band.

"I wouldn't bother counting it," said Black. "There's two hundred pounds there."

Holomek pulled out other items – old books, magazines, several pairs of shoes.

"I picked them up from the charity shop beneath your office, Chadwick. You could probably sell the lot on for a tenner."

Holomek turned the bag upside down, the contents cascading onto the carpet. "Fucking bastard!" he snarled. "Where's the fucking money!"

Black gave Holomek a level stare. "There is no money. There is no two million. There's nothing."

Chadwick, watching the scene unfold, got to his feet, his ruddy complexion washed away to a sickly grey, his mouth set under a disbelieving frown. "What's your game, Black?" he croaked. The opera timbre of his voice had disappeared.

The three were silent, waiting for Black to speak. He knew they wouldn't kill him until they heard why he was there. If there was a bigger play, then they would have been foolish not to find out about it, at the very least, for the purposes of self-preservation.

"He asked you a question, Black," said Kowalski, his voice quiet, menacing. "Did someone send you?"

Black turned to fix his full stare on Kowalski.

"Yes. I was sent."

"Who?"

Black's mouth curved into a slow smile. "The devil. Behind you."

Kowalski turned his head, just a fraction, towards the bay

windows. It was all the distraction Black needed. He flung the whisky glass at Kowalski, who jerked back instinctively, firing at the same time. The sound was sharp and loud, like a firecracker. The aim was wild, the bullet hitting a corner of the ceiling. Black leapt forward. Kowalski took aim again, but Black was on him, knocking his firing hand to one side. The pistol sounded again. Holomek, who had risen to his feet, spun backwards, to lie sprawling on the black leather chair, a bullet through his chin, the bottom of his jaw blown off and scattered in fragments on the pile of books.

Chadwick gasped, staggered back. Black and Kowalski rolled off the couch, crashing onto the coffee table, and onto the floor, Kowalski's hand gripped on the gun, Black's two hands clamped around Kowalski's wrist, trying to force the gun pointing away. Kowalski punched Black in the face, but there was no room for a full swing, the blow ineffective. The gun fired again, the bullet hitting the skirting on a wall.

They weaved backwards and forwards, first Black on top, then Kowalski. Black suddenly released one hand, punching Kowalski in the groin. Kowalski groaned, his grip on the pistol loosening. Black knocked it from his hand, sending it across the floor, and under one of the seats. Kowalski retaliated, hacking Black on the side of the neck using the edge of his hand. Black raised his shoulder, absorbing the blow, rolled, leaping to his feet, as did Kowalski, kicking away the remnants of the coffee table, creating space. They stood, facing each other. Black appraised him. About the same height – six-two, agile with hard muscle. Black aimed an apparently random blow at his head. Kowalski seized his wrist and lifted his knee at Black's groin. Black disengaged his wrist with a flick, caught Kowalski under the uplifted knee with his other hand and hoisted him backwards. Kowalski staggered. Black thrust forward, Kowalski losing his balance, and falling back on his side, onto the carpet.

Black leapt on him instantly, hammering his elbow against his face. Kowalski grunted in pain, the blow stunning him. Black twisted him onto his chest, seizing him in a two-armed clamp, pressed him face down, placed his knees on his shoulders, cupped his hand under his chin, jerked up, and snapped his neck.

Panting, Black rose to his feet. Chadwick hadn't moved, staring at the sequence of events, aghast, blood drained from his face. Before him lay two men, once his partners, now corpses. Before him, their killer – Adam Black.

"Let's have a chat," said Black.

47

Black retrieved the pistol from under the seat and turned his attention to Chadwick. He had to be quick. The gunshots would have attracted neighbours, pedestrians, anyone within a hundred yards. It wouldn't be long before the police were banging at the door.

"I didn't want any of this," Chadwick blurted. "You don't understand. I owed money to these... animals. I had no choice. If I didn't pay them, they threatened to kill my family. I have two children, Mr Black. What was I to do?"

"Go to the police?"

Chadwick gave his head an emphatic shake. "I couldn't do that," he muttered.

"Of course you couldn't. You're one of them. No different. When you sup with the devil."

"What do you want? Why are you here?"

"I recently bumped into a man with an exotic name. Teacup. He suggested I speak to you. I'm interested in an individual called Peter Grant. Maybe you know him?"

Chadwick raised his dark eyebrows, puffed out his cheeks.

"Peter Grant?"

Black waited. "He's a dangerous man," Chadwick continued. "I know very little about him."

Black raised the gun, pointing it directly at Chadwick's forehead. "If you don't answer my questions, I'll pull the trigger and lodge a bullet in your skull. Teacup said there was a deal going down. He said there was a lot of money involved. He said you knew all about it."

Chadwick nodded vigorously, the jowls on his face quivering.

"There is. But I'm only one piece of the jigsaw. Grant uses me to set up companies, with complicated structures. Shareholders who are companies, who themselves are operated by different companies. Directors who work under powers of attorney for overseas institutions. I set them up, get them registered, often with fictitious information. It's all part of the fog. Part of the snowstorm, to blind and confuse."

"Keep going."

"He wanted me to set up a company, to receive millions coming from overseas. The company structure was to be complex, but also, on the face of it, entirely legitimate. So, I did. I set up Abacus."

Black stared at Chadwick for several long seconds, absorbing this information.

"Abacus?"

Chadwick nodded. "But I'm only a part of the machine. I set up the framework. The funds still must go in and out. That takes lawyers. Lawyers who launder money."

"Who are the lawyers?"

"I have no idea, Mr Black. Peter Grant is careful in his dealings. Famously so. One hand is ignorant of the other. He's a secretive man. He goes out of his way to ensure that only he knows what his plans are. We have lunch occasionally at his restaurant, but he tells me very little beyond what I require to do my job." He blinked away sweat from his eyes, glancing from the pistol in Black's hand, to Black, back to the pistol. "If I may ask... what's your interest in him?"

"He murdered my family."

Chadwick swallowed, digesting this information. He drew a short ragged breath. "I don't know anything about that. You have to believe me. I'm only an accountant."

"An accountant who was happy to have me killed five minutes ago. Where is his restaurant?"

"Giovanni's. Royal Exchange Square."

"Thank you, Mr Chadwick. You've been very helpful. Time now to meet your friends."

Chadwick opened his mouth to speak, raising one arm as he did so. Black shot him once, through the forehead, as promised. An explosion of blood spattered the oil paintings on the wall behind him, as the bullet burst open the back of his head.

Black kept the gun, left the bodies where they lay, and departed the flat, out of the building, and melted into the night.

iovanni's. Black knew the place. He had dined there once, with clients. A million years ago. The prices on the menu were fashionably exorbitant. Too rich for Black. Too rich for most people. Yet it was always busy. You paid for the name, thought Black. You paid so that you could say you've been. If Black had his way, he'd burn the place down.

As Chadwick had mentioned, seconds before Black had fired a bullet into his skull, it was situated in the heart of Glasgow city centre, in Royal Exchange Square, a pedestrianised area of about two acres in size. The restaurant had an unassuming frontage. Walk by it quickly and you might miss it. Wedged in the middle of a row of upmarket establishments, ranging from a high-end jeweller to an academia bookshop, from coffee shops which charged eight pounds for a double-shot latte to a music shop specialising in bespoke violins, there was nothing to distinguish it from a thousand other restaurants. A dark-blue awning stretched over the front, allowing people to sit outside on white chairs at white tables, sheltered from the Scottish rain, guarded from the winter's chill by discreetly-placed patio heaters. At night, hundreds of tiny white fairy lights sparkled under the awning. Classical music played softly.

The interior had subtle warm lighting. It was never bright. When a person entered Giovanni's, they couldn't help but be impressed. A bar of dark polished oak on one side, and on it, silver ice buckets containing bottles of cold champagne. Behind the bar, a long gleaming gantry on frosted-mirror panelling, holding inverted bottles of every conceivable liquor. On the opposite side of the room, a step up to five booths with red leather seats. The walls were murals of Italian landscapes, all earthy colours, as was the high ceiling. Candelabras provided a soft subdued glow.

Past the bar and the booths was the restaurant proper. Circular booths, small intimate tables, larger tables. Candles flickered. More murals, of breathtaking quality. White tablecloths. The floor a deep wine-red carpet. Uniformed waiters moved briskly, quiet and attentive. Music played, just on the periphery of the senses. Always, the room was alive with the buzz of people talking, laughing, whispering.

This was the establishment which Grant owned. And it was here twice a week Grant enjoyed lunch, sitting at his table reserved for him and his entourage. Sometimes he dined on his own. Sometimes he dined with his associates. And when he did dine, he was rarely disturbed.

At one o'clock in the afternoon, the day following the incident at Macduff, Black entered Giovanni's. He ordered a soda water and lime and sat on a high stool at the bar. For a second, he observed his reflection in the mirrored wall behind the bar. The face which looked back was square-jawed, darkly handsome, black hair cropped short, yet it was not a face he recognised. This was a man from his past. A past stained with blood and spilled guts. Of war and death. A man who had killed with his bare hands. A man who could extinguish life without compunction.

A stone cold killer.

He attracted the attention of a bartender, a young man no older than twenty-one, who came over.

"Do you know Peter Grant?"

"Yes, I do, sir."

"I believe he dines here often."

The young man nodded. "He does. In fact, he's here now, in the restaurant, at his usual table."

"That's good to know. Where is his usual table?"

"In the rear corner, on the right-hand side as you enter. But he enjoys his privacy."

Black shrugged. "Who doesn't?"

The bartender tilted his head in agreement.

"Could you do something for me?" asked Black.

"Of course, sir."

Black leaned in closer. "I'd like to send over to Mr Grant's table a bottle of Moët. Could you do this for me? If you could mention that it's compliments of Adam Black, and if it's not an inconvenience, that Mr Black would like ten minutes of his time."

"I can certainly do that for you. But again, I have to say that Mr Grant likes his privacy. I can't guarantee he'll oblige."

"You can but try. You never know, I might get lucky."

49

Nathan had been asked to join Peter Grant for lunch at Giovanni's. He arrived, and joined him at the usual table, big enough for four people, a degree of privacy ensured by shoulder-high oak-panelled partitions. His uncle was already there, accompanied by his ever-present bodyguard, Thor.

He could tell immediately Grant was in an expansive mood. He'd already ordered, and a large dish of fresh plain oysters on a bed of crushed ice sat in the centre of the table. Beside it, a basket of assorted cut bread and on a little side trolley, Tabasco sauce, vinegar, sea salt, peppercorn and quartered lemon slices. Also on the table were bottles of still and sparkling water.

Grant had a napkin tucked behind his collar, as had Thor, and was in the process of downing oysters when he arrived.

"Better late than never." Grant laughed. "Enjoy." He nodded to a place which had already been set for him.

Nathan sat, and followed suit, putting on a napkin, and taking an oyster from the dish, and a piece of rough white bread from the basket, which he started to butter. "It's good to see you smiling again," he said. "Something's up. Care to tell me? Or should I guess?"

"Guess all you want," replied Grant.

"Maybe something to do with a large quantity of cash being transferred from Grand Cayman?"

"In one," said Grant. "There's a lot of money washed in, and right now it's in a safe place. Very soon it will be suitably cleaned up, moved on, and smelling fresh as the fucking daisies. And when that happens, the rollercoaster ride begins, because you'll be taking care of a good chunk of it. A sort of portfolio manager. Right up your street, Nathan, yes?"

Nathan nodded. "Absolutely." He had waited almost his entire adult life for this moment. "I won't let you down, Uncle Peter."

"Too fucking right, you won't. It's about time we put that degree of yours to a good cause." His voice dropped, almost to a whisper. "It was supposed to be you and Damian. Together, running the show. But not to be. Which means you'll have to fill his shoes as well. Think you're up for it?"

Nathan nodded again. "I am."

Grant's eyes narrowed. "We'll see. Play your cards right, our money could be doubled within two years. Maybe less. All legitimate. All clean as a fucking piper's whistle. So I think I can afford to have a smile on my face. It's been a long time coming. How are the oysters, Thor?"

Thor, who was sitting to his right, his massive shoulders almost taking up the length of his side of the table, gave a wide smile.

"Delicious," he said. "As good as any in Berlin." His accent was strong, his English broken. But Grant caught the gist.

"Fucking Berlin?" replied Grant, his face showing mock outrage. "Are you having a laugh? Let me tell you something. Listen close. Only this morning these very oysters you're shoving down your throat-hole were minding their business on some fucking rock, deep under the water, in a place called Loch Ryan.

They've been picked and delivered and served, all this morning. This is as fresh as you will ever get. This is as fresh as the fucking mountain air. No fucking frozen shit. Fucking Berlin! Unbelievable."

At that, Grant wriggled a short knife into the oyster shell, loosened the oyster, sprinkled on Tabasco sauce, tipped the shell into his mouth, and allowed the oyster to slide down his throat.

"Can't beat that," he said. "Class."

A waiter approached, holding a champagne bucket, and in it, a bottle of Moët & Chandon. The three men looked up.

"Sorry to trouble you, Mr Grant. Compliments of Adam Black. He was wondering if he could have ten minutes of your time."

Grant seemed to stare into space for a second. "Fuck me," he whispered. He glanced at Thor, and then said to Nathan. "The guy's got balls."

"No doubt about it." Nathan waited, aware his heart thumped like a drum in his chest. Waited to see what Peter Grant would do.

Grant picked up another oyster and started to knife free the meat from the shell. "Ask him over."

50

The waiter touched Black gently above the elbow. "Mr Grant has said that he'll be able to see you. If you follow me, I'll show you to his table."

"Thank you."

Black followed the waiter, past the bar and the raised booths, and into the restaurant. The waiter pointed discreetly to a table in the far corner, different from the others because it was enclosed on three sides by solid wood partitioning.

Black nodded. The waiter left. Black made his way over. He felt a strange dead calm. He was approaching the man who had orchestrated the murder of his family. Similarly, this same man was about to face the individual who had killed his only son. A gruesome symmetry, he thought. But the calmness he now experienced was not unknown to him. He had felt it before, on the field of battle, before a kill.

He got to the table. There were three men sitting at it. He recognised Grant immediately, from his pictures in the newspapers. The others he did not know, though the one facing him was unusually massive. Bodyguard.

Black addressed Grant. "May I join you?"

Grant tossed an empty oyster shell into a bowl. "Please do. Introductions – gentlemen, this is Mr Black. Mr Black, this is Thor, and my nephew, Nathan."

Black sat. The man before him, Peter Grant, was slim and tanned and very fit-looking. Black knew he was sixty-five, but he could have passed for a man twenty years younger – smooth skin, full head of grey hair, high cheekbones, solid chin. Shrewd green eyes. Eyes which did not miss the slightest detail.

"We meet at last," said Black. The big man opposite – Thor – leaned imperceptibly forward, placing two enormous hands on the table, palms down, fingers outstretched. He was saying – these hands will break your spine in two, Mr Black, if you make the tiniest sudden movement.

Grant flashed a smile, revealing perfect white teeth. "We were always going to meet, you and I. I never expected it to be here. I had other places in mind."

"Like where?"

Grant shrugged. "Less civilised places, shall we say."

"I understand completely. It was in such a place I bumped into your cousin – Tommy Teacup? Colourful name. Nice guy. He came at me once with a knife. I returned the compliment with a hammer."

The smile on Grant's face flickered. "A tragic loss. Losing family is a heavy burden to bear."

"I couldn't agree with you more. This is something we share. But in Teacup's case, it was most enjoyable. Like yourself, he was just another cheap gangster scumbag, so no one's going to miss him." Black's tone was almost affable. "And no one's going to miss you, when you die. And I'm hoping to bring that about soon."

A tremor seemed to pass through Grant's face. Black felt the big man opposite tense. But he knew, in this crowded place, he could do nothing. Safe ground.

Grant took a sip of mineral water. "I was just telling the boys here about the oysters. How only this morning they were picked off some rock, deep under the water. Must be a shit life, being an oyster." He took another sip, licked his lips with a pink darting tongue, and stared at Black, his gaze clear and unwavering. His voice lowered to a dry whisper. "That is where you will end up, my friend. Make no mistake. Deep under the water with the fucking oysters. Only you'll be dead, and the crabs will be chewing on your eyeballs. And to that I give my solemn fucking promise."

"I don't really know what a promise means from a cheap drug-dealing fuck," replied Black.

Grant smiled.

Black returned the smile. "By the way, Willard Chadwick passes on his regards. At least he would, if it weren't for the bullet I left in his face."

Grant cocked his head to one side, studying Black like an artist might study his new composition. "You're a busy fucker."

"I like to keep myself occupied. When I was in Afghanistan, I was always kept busy. We fought the Taliban. Mujahideen. Holy warriors, they called themselves. However you felt about them, they were tough bastards. They had the ability to invoke real fear in their enemies, including us. Real fear. This might interest you, Mr Grant, seeing as fear and intimidation are keywords in your line of business. Do you know how they achieved this?"

"Go on," said Grant. "Enlighten us with your wisdom."

"They had two advantages. One – they had no home. And so, like marauders, they attacked while always on the move. Like the corsairs of old. That's one difficult target. And two – they had nothing to lose, and so didn't care if they died. Most of these men came from annihilated families. Villages burnt, relatives murdered. The army can't cope with an enemy like that." It was

Black's turn to drop his voice to a whisper, like the rustle of dead leaves in the breeze.

"No one in the world can cope with an enemy like that," he added. "And those are the two advantages I possess. I have nothing to lose. And here's the good part. You'll never know when or where I'll strike. I'm not scared to die. I am your worst fucking nightmare, Mr Grant. And I am going to kill you. This is something you can count on."

A silence fell. Thor glanced at Grant for a sign, a signal. The other man – Nathan – sat motionless, suddenly pale, blood drained from his face. In a state of mild shock. He'd never heard anyone speak to his boss like that. Grant pursed his lips, as if pondering Black's words. Then he nodded, as if he'd come to some inward conclusion.

"You're a dead man, Black. Your death warrant is signed, sealed and delivered. It won't be quick, like your wife and daughter. Though I heard your daughter – Merryn? – begged for her life. Fucking begged. Must have been horrifying for the wee girl to see her mother shot down in front of her like a fucking bitch dog."

Black waited a few seconds. Then he spoke. "We'll meet again soon. Your oversized friend should dry his face."

Thor's big blunt features creased in puzzlement. Black picked up Grant's glass and flung the water into Thor's face.

"Easy, Thor!" snapped Grant.

"Easy, Thor." Black grabbed a long silver-handled fork, and stabbed Thor through one of his hands. It penetrated flesh, blood and bone, through the tablecloth and into the wood of the table, where it remained, standing upright.

Thor gave an abrupt shriek, staring wide-eyed at the utensil pinned clean through.

Black stood. "Hope I haven't spoiled your lunch." The

tablecloth under Thor's hand was blooming with a bright rosy stain.

"Don't get blood in your oyster. I'll catch up with you later, Mr Grant."

He gave the three seated men a polite nod, and left.

51

The Travellers Inn was a ten-storey block of rooms, a mile from the airport, in the middle of a retail park. A bland, unremarkable building. The ground floor comprised a compact restaurant, a small bar and lounge. Two receptionists manned the front check-in desk during the day. Shift change occurred at 7pm. A different receptionist sat by the desk during the night, together with a concierge. There was one lift and a set of stairs for those who liked the exercise, or for a fire escape. There were twenty rooms on each floor. The hotel was used mainly by business guests on short-stay trips, flying in and flying out. People came and went. Strangers passing. People ate their breakfast in silence, and then disappeared. The bar was used for a quick drink or two, but rarely for steady drinking bouts. It was functional. No frills.

Black had a room on the fourth floor. The main front entrance was locked at midnight, and entry was gained by electronic card – the same card used for entry to his room.

Nathan Grant had booked several rooms on the floor below, under fictitious names. An insurance convention in the city centre, he'd explained conversationally. This had been arranged only the day before. As a result of the meeting at Giovanni's, plans were suddenly accelerated, on instruction by an infuriated Peter Grant.

Nathan knew Black's room number. His uncle, mysteriously, had this information available, the source he'd kept to himself. Black hadn't bothered using a false identity, and Nathan wondered at his naivety. He assumed Black felt secure, which could only work to their advantage. The mission was brutally simple. Black was to be finished off. In his room. That night. Thor was to do the deed, accompanied by two others – hard men, reliable when it came to inflicting violence. Nathan was to wait in the car park. Easy. In theory.

He had been waiting in the car park adjacent to the main doors, close enough for him to watch people going in and out, but far enough away not to attract attention. The car – a black Vauxhall Astra, similar to a million others – was untraceable to him or anyone associated with him. In an hour, it would be left in a waste ground miles away, burnt out and abandoned. In the passenger seat, the massive figure of Thor, dressed in a suit and tie. At six foot seven, he sat with his head hunched against the car ceiling, a bandage wrapped around his hand – compliments of Adam Black. Thor was restless, barely able to contain his rage, muttering under his breath in his native tongue. Though the words *fucking bastard* were easy enough to understand. Two men sat in the back, also dressed smartly in suits. Insurance salesmen back late. Nothing untoward. All of them returning to their booked rooms.

Black had entered the building an hour earlier. It was time.

Despite the apparent simplicity, Nathan had his doubts. His stomach fluttered with nerves. He drummed his fingers on the steering wheel, anxious. The three men in the car were eminently capable, especially Thor. But Black was a formidable opponent. He thought back to the conversation earlier. Black had said he had nothing to lose. He wasn't afraid to die. Nathan suspected his uncle had never confronted an enemy like this. An enemy not motivated by money or power. An enemy who had only one thing on his mind. Revenge.

Thor picked up a black bag at his feet, which he opened, and pulled out three pistols, and three cylindrical-shaped objects. Silencers. He distributed them to the men in the back, one he kept, tucking it into a side holster hidden under his jacket, the silencer he put in his jacket pocket.

"Room eighty-three. Fourth floor. You ready for this?"

Thor grunted. "I'll break his fucking neck."

"No, you won't!" snapped Nathan. "No dramatics! No commotion. You understand? You go in, you shoot, you leave. It's supposed to be a simple sweet kill. In and out. Kill him, then go. I'll be waiting. Clean kill."

The muscle in Thor's jaw twitched. "No fun in that."

"It's not meant to be fun. It's meant to be a fucking job. Get focused, and get it done."

Nathan handed him the entry card. Thor took it, got out the car, followed by his two accomplices. Nathan watched them enter the hotel and took a deep breath.

52

The three men entered the main entrance of the hotel. The concierge was absent. The receptionist at the front desk barely raised his head, engrossed in his mobile phone. Black watched the trio enter from a quiet corner of the lounge. It was just after 1am, and he was the only person there. The bar had closed an hour earlier. He watched them take the lift. As soon as the doors had closed, he moved quickly, racing up the fire exit stairs. He had a good idea where they were going.

The three men reached the fourth floor. The hallway was like a thousand other hotel halls – beige carpet, pale nondescript wallpaper, forgettable framed prints on the wall. Decorated in colours of complete neutrality. They found Black's room. They unholstered their weapons, fitted the silencers, all executed quickly and in unison, performed by men competent in their business.

Thor stepped forward, and shot the handle off the door, the sound muffled, like a covered cough. He kicked the door open, and entered, followed closely by the others. It was dark, the curtains closed. There was one bed, a shape visible under the sheets. They positioned themselves around it, and fired, five shots each, five quick sharp bursts. Thor stretched over, pulled the sheets away. Pillows arranged in a row.

"Fuck!" shouted Thor.

Black appeared at the doorway, crouching, and entered the room. The three men jerked round. Black aimed his gun, fired once. Without the benefit of a silencer, and in the close confines of the room, the sound of the bullet discharging was like the crack of a firework. Like an explosion. One of the men flew backwards, top of his head blown off, colliding with Thor, both men falling to the ground. The other man aimed, fired, but it was dark, and Black was a moving target.

The bullet missed, a chunk of the wardrobe door above Black's head ripping away. Black rushed forward, firing as he ran, two bullets tearing through the man's throat, causing him to spin round, blood spattering on the walls and bed, like paint flicked from a brush. Black was out of bullets. Thor got to his feet, casting off his dead friend. He pointed his pistol, but Black was on him, batting the gun from his hand, sending it whirling. Thor punched Black hard in the face. His fist felt like concrete. Black was stunned, stumbling back on one foot. But he jabbed his fist out, catching Thor on the side of the head. Thor shrugged it off, twitching his head as if irritated by a fly. Black followed up instantly with a right-handed blow on Thor's chin. It had zero impact. Like hitting a tree trunk.

Suddenly Thor leapt forward, roaring as he did so, disconcertingly fast for a man his size, both arms wide. Black punched again at the face, striking the left eye, but was caught in a bear hug. He raised a knee, pressing it against Thor's pelvis to keep from being crushed. Thor tightened his hold. He was grinning.

"Gonna squeeze the fucking life out of you."

Black had never encountered such strength. In three seconds, his spine would snap. With a gut-wrenching effort, he pulled back against Thor's grip, using his knee as leverage. The grip loosened. Black used the moment to swing his head in and inflict a crunching headbutt, square on Thor's mouth. He felt teeth crack. Thor released his hold, stepped back, shook his head, stepped forward again, raising his arms. Black struck out at his left eye; a massive hand hacked at his neck. Black sidestepped, his shoulder absorbing the blow. He leapt forward, like a rugby tackle, thrusting his body against Thor's stomach, which was ribbed with muscle and hard as oak.

Thor staggered back, kept his feet, pulled up a knee, battering Black on the chest. Black caught hold of the knee, wrenched it to one side, twisting ligaments. Thor grunted in pain, but reached over and somehow caught Black in an arm lock. Black allowed his knees to go limp, then leapt backwards in a kind of mad half-somersault, his arm pulled free. Thor lost balance, tottered back against the closed curtains; Black sprang forward, kicking Thor hard in the abdomen. Thor doubled over, but lashed out with an arm, catching Black on the ribs. Black sucked his breath in, winded, drove his elbow into Thor's throat. Thor released a rattling gasp, choked, momentarily distracted. Black stood on something – the pistol, once owned by the man with half his brains on the bedroom wall. He snatched it up, just as Thor came stumbling towards him. Black raised the pistol and fired once, at point-blank range into Thor's face. In the split second between the discharge of the bullet and its impact between Thor's eyes, Black had a fleeting image of Thor's features caught in horrified disbelief.

Thor was knocked off his feet, the back of his head a sudden eruption of blood, the force propelling him through the curtains, and through the fourth-storey window. Black leaned over – below, Thor lay crumpled in the car park, all limbs and blood, head smashed to splinters, neck twisted at a gruesome angle.

Black saw a car speed off. Good idea, he thought.

53

Grant did not sleep that night. He was in his conservatory, shrouded in shadow. He needed to hear Nathan say those sweet words, pronouncing Adam Black's death. He needed to hear it badly, like an itch he couldn't scratch. Since their meeting at Giovanni's, the whole thing had cranked up several notches. The insults had nettled him, but insults couldn't hurt. But when Black said he'd met the accountant – Willard Chadwick – then matters became suddenly pressing.

Chadwick was a loose-lipped bastard at the best of times. God knows what he'd told Black. Grant couldn't take any chances. He had to move things forward. And the only way Grant could be assured of Black's non-interference was to kill him, once and for all. Remove him, like a cancer, before his infection spread.

The phone on the armrest of his chair vibrated. Grant immediately picked up. The sound was Nathan's breathless voice, agitated, and Grant knew instantly things were bad.

"It's a fucking mess," gasped Nathan. "Thor's dead. Lying in the car park with his head smashed open. The other two are probably dead. I couldn't wait. The whole thing's a mess!"

Grant hung up. He gazed out at his exquisite gardens, illuminated by soft blue and green lanterns, their delicate hues and subtle shades offering no consolation. He inhaled deeply, took a long slow exhalation, calming himself. He felt no remorse for the loss of his bodyguard. Such a man was expendable. His sudden absence was an irritation, at worst. Grant dialled another number, which was answered immediately, and Grant issued his instructions.

54

Black headed straight back to his hotel. His *other* hotel. He had kept the room at the Travellers Inn but had checked into another one immediately upon his return from Macduff. His intuition had paid off, his suspicions confirmed.

He got to the hotel, a place called Express Lodges on the south side of Glasgow, clean and relatively cheap, and immediately retreated to his room on the second floor, where he examined his wounds – bruising on his ribs and neck, but nothing serious. A little discomfort for a few days. His enemies had fared much worse. His shoulder was stiffening; his lip swollen where the man called Thor had struck him. Nothing catastrophic. Certainly nothing that would slow him down.

It had been proved to be a profitable encounter. He had picked up a couple of handguns, complete with silencers. Two Glocks. Hand cannons. Powerful, effective, costly. Grant was sparing no expense in orchestrating Black's demise.

He showered and fell onto his bed. It was 3am. In the last seven days, he had killed eight men. Men who meant nothing to him. But he surmised Peter Grant was beginning to get the picture. Adam Black was not going away.

He kept the bedside light on and stared at the ceiling. He was dog-tired. His mind drifted, to his wife and daughter. Their faces wavered before him, shadowy and unclear. He could not picture them exactly. An expression, a smile, a side glance, laughter. He had failed them, and for that, his guilt was profound and inconsolable. Innocents allowed to be slaughtered by a psychopath. Black, even in his exhaustion, felt his anger roil. Wild raw anger. Only satisfied when he'd ripped Grant's heart from his body. Black fell into a fitful sleep.

He woke, not to his alarm, but to the sound of his mobile phone. Only one person had his number. He looked at the name displayed on the screen, hesitated, then answered. "Simon?"

"I thought you wouldn't pick up."

Black was instantly alert. It was Simon Fletcher, his partner, his voice agitated, panicked. "What's wrong, Simon?"

"Everything. Where are you?"

"In a safe place. You don't need to worry about me."

He heard Fletcher's heavy ragged breathing on the other end, as if he'd been running. Black recognised the sound, an echo of an earlier encounter. Fletcher had shown the same nervous symptoms when he'd described discovering the body of John Wilson, hanging by the neck in his front living room.

"We have to meet. Please."

"What's wrong, Simon?"

"Tonight. Say seven? They've taken her."

Black had to think. His skin prickled. He replied, an edge to his voice. "Who are *they*?"

"The people you've upset. They've said they'll kill my family." A deep shuddering breath. "They've got Katie, for fuck's sake. Please, Adam. I don't know what the hell's going on, but they said if I call the cops, they'll kill her. They'll kill her! What am I supposed to do!"

Black was still tired, it wasn't yet dawn, and he had killed three men only hours earlier. He forced himself to concentrate. "Katie?" She was Simon's younger daughter. Twelve years old. About to start secondary school.

Breathing. Then, "They've said they're going to kill her." Simon's tone of voice changed to a leaden monotone, as if all the life had been sucked out of him. "Did you hear that? Kill my daughter. Unless I find a way to..."

"What?"

"... to get you to hand yourself over. I need to call the police. This is crazy."

"Don't call anyone," replied Black, his voice deadpan, emotionless. "If you do, then you're right. Your daughter will die. And they'll kill you too. It's me they want. We'll meet. At the office for seven. Don't speak to anyone. I'll come up with a plan. We'll get through this, Simon. I promise."

Black hung up. The stakes in the game had suddenly been raised. But it was a game he was prepared to play.

55

The offices of Wilson, Fletcher and Co. comprised the entire first floor of a large block of shops and offices just off Renfield Street, in Glasgow city centre. Nineteenth-century Victorian architecture at its best – smooth red sandstone walls, gable roof, high-arched windows. Inside, a spacious suite of rooms; six separate offices for partners and paralegals, a client meeting room which doubled as the library, a secretarial room, a common room, two toilets, and showers. A small brass plaque displayed on the wall beside the main entrance was the only feature advertising their existence. That, and white lettering on the first-floor windows. The ground floor was a Spanish tapas restaurant, a trendy wine bar, and a sports shop. There was an elevator, and stairs, and a single concierge manned the front reception until five thirty. There were two floors above Wilson Fletcher, consisting of accountants, surveyors, and two insurance agents.

Black parked his car a quarter mile away and walked. He was a half hour early, and well-armed. In each coat pocket was a Glock. He had dispensed with the silencers; they might reduce the noise of a gunshot, but accuracy was affected. If Black fired, he needed certainty. The bullet had to hit the target. He carried three knives, one in his inside jacket pocket, one in his trouser pocket, and a switchblade tucked under his sock, stuck to his skin with tape. He was a walking arsenal. He approached the entrance to his offices warily. It was six-thirty on a Thursday evening, and it was cold and already getting dark. The place was quiet. It would get busier in a couple of hours, when people roused themselves for dinner and drinking.

Black scanned the street. Nothing untoward. It was possible that a shooter was nestled on a rooftop or aiming through an open window from an adjacent office. He scrutinised the surroundings. There were no rooftops allowing a clear shot. The windows in the block opposite were all closed, as far as he could tell. Still, he kept to the shadows, close to the wall, increasing his pace to a march, nerves tingling. He kept his hands in his coat pocket, cradled round the pistols. Cars were parked on either side of the street, all empty. He braced himself for a sudden door opening, the crack of a semi-automatic discharging in his direction. He reached the front entrance. He had a key. He unlocked the heavy wooden door, entered, senses heightened. So far, so good.

The lights were on in the front reception area, which was not unusual. As expected, the counter was unmanned. Black stopped, straining to hear the slightest sound, the scrape of movement. Silence.

He daren't take the lift. He took the stairs, creeping up on his toes, hugging the banister, soft as shadow. He held a Glock in his right hand.

He got to the first floor. No sign of anyone. He opened the fire door and emerged into a carpeted hall. On a wall was the name of his firm, in big, bold black letters, and beside it, the only door in and out of the suite of offices. He experienced a brief strange sensation when he saw the firm's name. A memento from a past life far removed from the present. A life he knew he could probably never return to, and now he was a spectator, raking over the ruins of his previous existence.

He paused, straining to hear something. *Anything.* But there was no sound. He crouched, gently opened the door. He crept into the main reception area. The lights were all on. He now had both pistols out, not unlike the gunfighters in a western movie. A sound drummed in his head – his heartbeat.

The place was neat, orderly. Everything in its place. Life went on, he mused.

A sound from the conference room, down a corridor only twenty yards away. A sob. Then glass breaking. Nerves stretched, Black sidled down the corridor. He reached the conference room door, half-open. He gently nudged it wider, both guns pointed forward. He entered. Nothing had changed; the shelves of law books, the long rectangular conference table, where he'd sat a thousand times with clients discussing matters legal, the air heavy with the remnants of fresh coffee. It all seemed a million light years away. Sitting at the far end of the table, smoking a cigarette, was Simon Fletcher. On the table in front of him was an ashtray already full of cigarette stubs and a half-empty whisky bottle. Shards of broken glass glittered across the surface of the table.

Fletcher was staring at an adjacent wall, surrounded by smoke, seemingly deep in his own thoughts.

"Hello Simon."

Fletcher jerked round. "Adam. You startled me."

Black walked round the table, to sit two up from Fletcher, his back to the book shelves, facing the door.

"You look terrible." Fletcher stubbed his cigarette out, and lit another one with a cheap plastic lighter, his hands noticeably trembling.

"Thanks. You're shaking."

"No fucking wonder." He took a deep inhalation and fixed his gaze on Black. "The world's on fire."

"The world's always on fire," replied Black. "You just live with it."

"Just live with it? Really? Is that what you're doing?"

"Your daughter. Grant's got her. That's what you said."

Fletcher picked up the bottle and took a gulp of whisky, face contorting. "I hate this stuff. Tastes like shit." He stretched the bottle over to Black. "Take some."

"People keep offering me whisky. No thank you."

"How long have we known each other? Twenty years? Twenty-five? It all merges together, don't you think? Until you forget."

"Forget what?"

"Forget what's right and wrong."

"It can be a narrow line. So, your daughter?"

Fletcher fixed a glassy gaze on Black. "You must have crossed that narrow line before. In Afghanistan. Where there's no rules. Don't say you haven't."

"There are always rules, Simon. No matter where you are. Either on the outside, or in your heart. It just depends on whether you're prepared to break them."

"That's one fucking glib answer."

"It's the truth."

"This whole fucking thing has got so out of hand."

"What's got out of hand, Simon?"

Fletcher wrenched his gaze away, to stare at the floor.

"This!" He waved his arm vaguely around him. "Everything!"

Black remained silent for several seconds. Then he spoke, his voice soft, quiet.

"Have you always worked for Grant?"

A noise from outside, near the entrance. A scrape of

movement, the almost undetectable padding of careful footsteps. Now Black heard low, urgent whispering.

"I'm sorry, Adam. But it must come to this. There was no other way."

"I'm sorry too. But there's always another way." He pointed one of the guns towards the door of the room, keeping one eye on the entrance, the other on Fletcher.

"I heard the name Abacus in the living room of an accountant called Chadwick," said Black. "It struck a chord. I was sure I'd seen a file in your room with the same client name. But I didn't want to believe it. And then last night. Only you knew I was staying at the Travellers Lodge. But I still didn't want to believe it. And John Wilson? What happened there?"

Fletcher looked down, staring at the broken glass, his face slack. "John?" Fletcher gave a hollow laugh. "Greedy bastard is how I'd describe John Wilson. He found out. When he did, he wanted a piece. A rather large piece. A man like Peter Grant doesn't tolerate things like that. Not for long. But you know all about that. You've already tasted the breadth of his spite."

Black ignored the remark. "John found out about Abacus. He found out that you were about to launder millions, and he wanted his cut."

Black glimpsed a shadow at the door. He tried to keep his voice under control. He needed a crucial piece of information. "And the cops in the police station. That night in the interview room. DI Patterson was waiting for you. Waiting for instructions."

Fletcher nodded, his speech slurred at the edges. "Grant wanted you out on the streets. He has many powerful friends in high places, and so it was arranged. The fucking wizard with his wand. He waves it, and magic happens. No way were you being charged. Grant wanted revenge. And he wanted a free rein to carry it through. He didn't want the criminal justice system getting in the way. I was the bearer of this message. Grant knew it was you who killed his son a half hour after you'd done it. As soon as the cops had you in the cells, and they knew who you were, they phoned Grant. And Grant phoned me. You want to hear something funny?"

"Sure." Black's nerves tingled. He heard voices. He reckoned there were four, maybe five men, waiting for him. No doubt bristling with firepower.

"Grant thought you'd killed his son, to get to him. Because we work in the same firm. He thought you knew about his little scheme, and were trying to muscle in." He waved his hands, whisky sploshing from the bottle. "But the whole thing was one big fucking coincidence. A random act of God! I told him. I fucking told him. The whole thing is so fucked up!"

"Sure it is. What's in it for you, Simon? What about your wife, your kids?"

"I get fifteen per cent of forty million from all those bank accounts. Do the maths. I can buy a new future. The wife and kids, well, I'll find a new woman, and get new kids, somewhere where there's a sandy beach and a warm breeze and cocktails by the sea."

"And you can swim with fucking dolphins. So how? The money's laundered through the firm's client account. All under my nose?" Black was speaking quickly. Time was running out.

Fletcher took a deep drag. "I'm the cash-room partner, Adam. It's me who checks the accounts. This whole thing's been planned for months. Even if you'd been in the office, the money would have passed through our account, and you'd be none the wiser. As it happened, you had certain distractions to keep you occupied. The accounts will be audited by the Law Society six months from now. By then I'll be well away, the money dispersed, and Peter Grant untouchable."

"And I'd be left, looking at ten years for money laundering. Thanks for that."

"You're what's called collateral damage. It's all academic. Why the fuck did you have to kill Grant's son!"

"Shit happens." Black looked at Fletcher, square on. "If the money's in our client account, let's split it. Fuck Peter Grant. Fuck them all. With that type of money, we could disappear."

Fletcher gave a bitter laugh. "Seriously? I don't have a death wish, Adam. Not like you. The money will be gone tomorrow, to various sources, and then it's all washed clean."

"And what about Jennifer and Merryn? What about them? Where do they feature?"

Fletcher took another swig from the whisky bottle.

"I had no idea he would go that far. I really didn't."

Black nodded. "I understand. A piece of advice. Don't call someone 'collateral damage' when they have a gun. I'm sorry, Simon."

Black shot Fletcher twice through the chest, the noise loud and sharp. Fletcher flew back off his chair, in a half-somersault. Black stood, stepped forward, and emptied another bullet through his head, to make sure. Fletcher had given him the information he needed.

It had been worth the risk.

Now he had Grant where it hurt.

56

Nathan and six men were grouped outside the conference door, each carrying a semi-automatic pistol, including himself. He was unaccustomed to this side of the business. The gun felt like a foreign object in his hand. A million miles from the cloistered ambience of the university library. But orders were orders. He was here. He had a job to do. No way was Black going to get out of this. The trap was sprung. Black was a dead man.

He heard the shots – three in all. It was hard not to hear them. They echoed throughout the office like three thunderclaps. Nathan motioned one of his men to peek round the conference door. The man did so, just a fraction. There was an immediate gun shot, the door bouncing back, the bullet from Black's gun shredding it, and in the process eviscerating the side of the man's face, felling him instantly.

"Shit!" exclaimed Nathan.

"Shit's the word," responded Black, from the far corner of the room. "I've got plenty more bullets. You'd better phone Grant. Tell him Fletcher's dead. Tell him I killed the fucker."

"We're here for you, Black! Whether Fletcher's alive or dead, makes no difference. That's the way it has to be."

"It might make a difference to Grant. Without me, he can't get his money. Tell him, I know about Abacus. Tell him, the funds are in our client account. Tell him, only two people in the whole fucking world know the account password. Simon Fletcher, who lies at my feet with several bullets in his body. And me. Tell him that – and if you're still okay about killing me, then you've signed your own death warrant."

Nathan listened, trying to take in this sudden new information, head spinning with indecision. Was Black trying to play him? His uncle was secretive; Nathan did not know the full extent of his business interests. But he was aware of massive amounts of money moving imminently. He was aware it involved a company called Abacus. And he knew Simon Fletcher was involved. Now Fletcher was dead.

Nathan pressed speed dial on his mobile, and the sharp tone of his uncle answered.

"Well? Is it done?"

"We've got him cornered in his office. He's not going anywhere."

"That's not what I asked!" barked Grant. "Why don't you just answer the fucking question, Nathan. So, it's not done. In which case, why are you phoning me?"

"There's been a development."

"Which is?"

"He says he's killed Simon Fletcher. He says only he and Fletcher know, knew, the password for the client account. What do you want me to do?"

A silence followed. Nathan felt he could almost hear the gears in his uncle's brain click and grind.

"He killed his own partner," said Grant at length, his voice surprisingly calm. "His best friend. I didn't see that. He's full of surprises."

Nathan waited.

"Don't kill him. Capture him. I need him alive. I need to trust you can do that."

Grant disconnected. Nathan contemplated the situation he was in and thought – how the hell do you capture a man like Adam Black?

57

Nathan ushered his men back from the door, which was drooping off its hinges as a result of Black's gunshot. And on the floor, the man with half his head blown away, also courtesy of Black's gunshot.

Nathan crept forward. "I've spoken to Peter Grant! He needs to talk to you. You won't be harmed. He just wants to talk."

"You give me your solemn promise?"

Nathan was not oblivious to the sarcasm. But he had to respond. "Of course."

"Let me think about that."

Suddenly the crash of a window breaking. Nathan hesitated. They were only one floor up. It was not inconceivable that Black could leap out a window and survive the landing.

"Fuck!"

He gestured his men in, five armed individuals, Nathan following up behind. The window was gone, shards of glass scattered on the carpet. A chair was toppled beside it. One of his men rushed over to the space, and looked down.

"Is he there?" Nathan asked

"I'm right here," came a soft voice from the opposite corner of the room.

Everyone spun round, to be met by Black, crouched in the shadows, a Glock in each hand, pointing right at them. He fired, moving at the same time, shielded by the heavy wooden table. Nathan watched, stricken, as three of his men dropped to the floor, torsos riddled with bullets. The others got to get some shots off, but Black was a moving target, and the shots went wide. Nathan leapt to the ground, taking shelter under the table. Black darted past the door, and out of the room.

"Get the fuck!" screamed Nathan.

The two remaining men ran after him, to be shot instantly as they left the room, each in the head. Black had not run. He had waited for them in the corridor outside.

"Jesus," muttered Nathan. He was no fighter. Far from it. He was the one who dispensed orders, at the behest of his uncle. This wasn't the place for him. He was not the one to get involved at close range. He was so scared, he felt his bowels might loosen right there and then.

He waited, watching under the table for Black to enter. Maybe he could shoot his feet, he thought. But if he missed...

He waited, one minute, two. He raised his head above the edge of the table. Nothing. Silence. He stood, body held in exquisite stillness. The place was carnage. Bodies and blood everywhere, glass and smashed furniture. Shredded books. Bullet punctures in the walls.

Nathan realised he had been holding his breath. He took a long exhalation.

His mobile phone suddenly buzzed, breaking the eerie silence. He jerked his hand up and looked at the name showing on the screen. It was Peter Grant.

58

We train you for primarily two reasons. To kill. And to endure.

Black waited by the conference room door – or what remained of it – pressed against the wall, gun aimed at head height. Two men ran out, and it was a simple double tap, almost execution style, and they both dropped. Black couldn't wait any longer. The gunshots and the window smashing would not have gone unnoticed. He reckoned he had about five minutes to leave the building and get far enough away to avoid getting caught up in the mayhem to follow – from either more hired thugs, or the police. He had just dispatched six men, and his partner, Simon Fletcher. He felt no guilt. He knew Simon's wife and kids, had bought Christmas presents for them, spent holidays with them. But at least they were alive. Black's family no longer enjoyed that experience.

He left the offices, taking the stairs again, moving warily, watchful, but the way seemed clear. He got to the main reception area. Everything seemed normal. Nothing was out of place. Who would have thought a gunfight had erupted in the floor above?

He waited at the entrance. The double doors were closed. They were solid, without any glass panelling. No one could see in, but then he couldn't see out. He took a deep breath, opened the door a fraction, then wider. The way was clear. He slipped out, closing the door behind him, and started walking down the street, casually, as if he were going nowhere in particular, both guns tucked back in his coat pockets.

A jogger came up towards him, appearing as if from nowhere. Black tensed but kept moving. The jogger was running at speed, wearing a dark-green hoodie, face hidden in shadow. Black slowed as he approached. The jogger ran straight by. Black stopped, turned, watching him go. He did not see the people in the parked car. The car door opened. Black spun round, but too late! A man fired something directly at his chest – two darts pierced his coat, connected by conductors to a hand weapon. A taser. Suddenly an electric current coursed through Black's muscle fibres, causing instant contraction. He was still conscious when he fell, but his muscles were locked rigid. He hit the pavement hard, entombed in his own body.

The man holding the gun loomed over him. Black looked into a face he recognised – Peter Grant.

"You don't send a fucking boy to do a man's job."

Black heard car doors opening and shutting. He was lifted quickly by four men and carried over to the boot of a Range Rover. He was bundled in, his coat and jacket removed. One of the men produced a cosh and rendered a fearful blow to the back of his head.

Black lost consciousness, his world tumbling into oblivion.

59

You don't send a fucking boy to do a man's job.

The words repeated themselves over and over in his mind. He was not awake. But he was not unconscious. He was in a grey place in between.

A sound penetrated his head. Laughter. Or at least a sound which resembled laughter. It faded in and out of his consciousness, one moment distinct, next a faint echo, a glimmer of a sound. He swallowed back a tidal wave of pain.

He had been careless.

He was going to die.

He cracked his eyes open a fraction, finding the light almost blinding. He clenched his teeth against waves of nausea. And pain – a throbbing pain, beating like a base drum in the middle of his head.

Memories seeped back, at first slowly, then like a flood. The paralysing pain of electrocution from the taser. Being grappled and bundled into the back of a car. The crack of the cosh on his skull. He swallowed, but even that simple act was painful. His throat was parched. He tried to move, but discovered he was bound. He surveyed his position in an almost detached fashion.

He was sitting on a chair, hands tied behind his back painfully tight with what felt like rope, his ankles bound to the chair legs. His shirt had been removed, as had his socks and shoes. His knives discovered and taken, he thought ruefully. His eyes gradually adjusted to the light, and he began to make sense of his surroundings.

He was in a large, heavily-furnished room. To his left was a log fire, set beneath a dark oak surround, the flames reduced to dull embers. Black noted a poker was resting on a metal grille, one end burrowed deep in the smouldering heat. Everywhere was wood. Wooden flooring, with scattered rugs; walls of deep oak panelling; high wooden ceiling with dark beams. The place looked cluttered – leather couches and tapestried chairs and small tables, positioned in no particular order. In fact, they had been pushed back, he realised, to provide clear space around him. For fun and games, he thought grimly.

The room was lit by various lamps and downlighters from the ceiling. In a corner was a grand piano, polished until the wood shone, gleaming. Windows and wide French doors stretched across almost the length of a far wall, heavy drapes at each end drawn open and fastened by tiebacks. Above the fireplace was a large painting of Peter Grant, gazing into the middle distance, a shotgun resting against his shoulder, dressed like a country squire in a brown three-piece tweed suit, standing with a Labrador at his feet, and a mountain in the distance, and a blue sky above.

Black licked his lips. They felt cracked and swollen. His whole face felt painful. Perhaps someone had already vented their anger on him, while he was unconscious. It felt like it.

His thoughts drifted back, to another time, another world. Old memories surfaced.

Dungeons deep under a prison in Iraq, carved out of the cold stone. Starving, waking up every morning to a ritual beating. Hanging by the wrists for hours on end. Every so often a mock execution. Waterboarding, just for fun. Watching beheadings of other inmates. He had been trained to endure. The SAS understood that in their particular line of business, capture was a real possibility. Training had included psychological and physical torture in simulated conditions. But despite how harsh those conditions were, ultimately, it was just pretend. No one died. Nothing could prepare a soldier for the real thing. For Black, facing death as he did then daily, the fear of dying became something he grew accustomed to, until he was able to manage it, contain it. And once contained, it gradually changed to a new and vibrant emotion. Rage. He escaped from that hellhole, and in the process, took great pleasure in slitting the throats of three of his guards. He wondered if he would be so lucky this time.

Laughter again, from another room. Two men entered. One he knew he'd seen before. He picked through his memory, trying to place him. It was like trying to swim through a fog. He remembered. The man in the BMW. The man who'd been waiting outside his house in Eaglesham . The man whose friend Black had stabbed through the eye with a key. The other he also recognised. Vaguely. A tinge of recollection. A face he'd seen in a room in a police station an eternity ago, when his bloodstained clothes had been removed; when he'd just killed Damian Grant outside a pub in Eaglesham. A burly, round-faced man with hair so fine, he looked bald. The man who never smiled.

DS Lomond.

"You're awake," said the BMW man.

Black rolled his tongue around his teeth. "I'm in a nightmare. I'm looking at two fat goblins. Can I have some water?"

"What the fuck did you just say!" shouted Lomond, specks of saliva flying off the corners of his mouth.

"Easy, Jack," said the other one. "He's a lippy bastard, but just ignore it. He won't be lippy for long."

BMW Man stepped close to Black, and leaned over him, his face six inches away. "Do you remember me?"

"How could I forget, with a face like yours."

"Do you remember what you did to my pal? He lost an eye. He lost a fucking eye! Now he has to wear a fucking patch. He's not very pleased. He is what you would describe as *fucking outraged!* He wants me to pass on this message – that when Mr Grant is finished doing what he has to do, he wants me to scoop out your eyeballs with a fucking spoon, and put them on a key ring, so he'll have nice memories of you."

Black gazed up at the man looming over him. "Here's a message for your handsome one-eyed pal." Black spat in the man's face.

The man recoiled, lips curled back in a mixture of anger and disgust. But he did not retaliate. He daren't, probably on the orders of Grant, surmised Black. He wasn't to be critically damaged, otherwise he wouldn't be able to talk. And Black knew that Grant was desperate for him to talk.

Another door opened, somewhere in the vicinity behind Black. Eight men now entered the room, forming a semi-circle round where Black sat. One of them was Peter Grant. Another was Nathan.

Grant fixed Black with a long stare. "A bit different from Giovanni's. Doesn't quite have the same ambience."

"Not quite the same. I'll bet the food's a lot cheaper. Can I have a glass of water?"

"Of course. Nathan, get the man some water."

Nathan left.

Grant stepped closer, and leant forward, his hands on his knees, scrutinising Black's face. "You're not looking so good, old pal. Looking a bit 'fucked up'. That's what happens when you start meddling about in my business affairs."

"I started meddling when you decided to murder my wife and daughter. A fairly natural reaction, wouldn't you say?"

Grant shrugged. "You deserved all you got. As did they. The scales were balanced."

Nathan returned with a tall glass tumbler of water and placed it at Black's lips. Black drank greedily, Nathan slowly tilting the glass as Black gulped it down.

"Now then," continued Grant. "Refreshments are over. You know exactly why you're here. My money is in your firm's client account. You very rudely killed off the only means by which the money was to be transferred, namely Simon Fletcher. That deal is now, like yourself, fucked up. I need the money back. So please. Return it to me."

"Sorry about the deal going sour," said Black. "What was it – a fraudulent land transfer? From one company to another. Another layer added, to make the laundering harder to discover. And then what? Closing the companies down, dissolving them. By then the money has been moved on, to where? A hundred other companies, in legit transactions? And so, the Peter Grant drug and extortion fund is cleaned up and accessible, and all remnants of proceeds of crime almost impossible to trace. So sad that I ruined it all for you. Now it's a bonus if you even get your money back. Especially when the police start crawling over one major fucking crime scene. I lost count of the dead bodies. Let me guess – the money goes back to where it originated? A Swiss bank account? Virgin Islands?"

"Cayman Islands, seeing as you asked. And you've ruined nothing. A setback is all. A blip. Bent lawyers are almost as common as bent coppers. And they're as common as fucking turds in a sewer. I'll find another firm somewhere, some classy corporate outfit that looks good on the outside, but on the inside is desperate for cash. In Fletcher's case, it was sheer greed."

"And Wilson?"

"That grasping little fuck? I enjoyed having him killed. Just your luck to be a partner in a law firm full of villains. Now both your partners are dead. And here we are. What is the password, please? If you tell me now, then it will be much easier for you."

"You'll let me go, of course."

"We're grown-ups, you and I. You know that can't happen. But I could unleash Badger on you, and then the whole thing becomes messy."

"You have such cute names for each other. Badger. Tommy Teacup. What's yours – Drug-Dealing Filthy Scumbag?"

"You've already met Badger," replied Grant, his tone almost affable. "He's the one who wants to kill you because you blinded his pal. We could all leave the room, and give him two minutes, and then come back, and ask you again."

"Good idea. Badger will kill me, and you know it. And then you can say goodbye to all your hard-earned cash. How much by the way – forty million? More? If you don't get that back, then I wonder how long the Peter Grant empire will last."

"Wonder all you want," said Grant. "You're going to tell me the password. Looks like we're doing it the hard way. For you, that is. Enjoyable for me."

He flicked a glance at one of the men, nodding towards the fire. The man knew what it meant. All planned, thought Black. A structured torture.

The man picked up a towel that had been folded by the hearth and used it to wrap around the handle of the poker resting in the embers. He pulled the poker out. It glowed. He handed it to Grant, who raised it up in the air, gazing at it, swivelling it in his hand, as if he were admiring a piece of artwork.

"Scream all you want, Mr Black. You're a guest of my hunting lodge, which is in the middle of fucking nowhere. Though if you're interested, you're in the heart of the Cairngorms. Red squirrels and grouse and Scottish wilderness, and not much fucking else. No one will hear you, so scream, my friend. There's no shame."

Black tensed. Grant lowered the fire poker to an inch from Black's chest. It didn't touch the skin, but still it felt like he was on fire. He gritted his teeth, clenched his fists.

"I've always been impressed by the medieval forms of torture," continued Grant, addressing the men around him. "Back then, they did not fuck about. Branding was popular. As a precursor, before the real stuff. So, here's a precursor, Mr Black. Enjoy."

He placed the red-hot iron gently on the centre of Black's chest. Black groaned. The pain was searing. Grant slowly drew the iron down, then across and around his nipple. Black took quick gasping breaths, mind-jarring pain coursing through every particle of his body.

Grant lifted the iron, admiring his handiwork. "Give Mr Black another drink of water. I think he needs more light refreshment during the interval."

Nathan nodded, and left.

"Did you enjoy that?" Grant asked.

Black swallowed back a sudden feeling of nausea. He shook his head, as if the act would clear his mind of the pain, which it didn't. "Loved it."

"That's nice. We have all evening." Grant was wearing a dark-blue leather jacket, which he removed, and placed over the back of a chair. "This is hot work, though a lot hotter for you. What's the password?"

Black brought his gaze up to Grant, his vision blurred, the

world out of focus. "The password is – goodbye forty million pounds."

Grant sighed, and almost casually rested the poker on Black's right shoulder, where he let it sit. The skin sizzled. Black released a low moan. He could smell his own burning flesh.

"That's not very funny," said Grant. "For a man in your position. This can go on all night. So, stop fucking about. Or the pain you are feeling right at this moment will be like paradise compared to later."

Grant kept the poker on Black's shoulder blade for another five seconds, then lifted it away. Black gasped.

Nathan had returned, and again placed the lip of the glass gently to Black's mouth. Black drank in tentative sips.

Grant returned the poker to one of his men, who replaced it into the glowing red embers. "Get more logs in. Let's get a roaring fire."

60

Nathan watched silently as the torturing progressed through the evening. Every so often he was asked by his uncle to fetch water, which did not irk him in the slightest. He was glad of it. The spectacle was not enjoyable to watch. Not for him. The others were relishing it. But Nathan knew how this was going to play out. Black would never talk. And if that happened, then forty million was a lot to lose. Black would die, and the password with him. Then Nathan dreaded how his uncle would react.

Every so often, Black would slip into unconsciousness, and then the water was used to splash his face and bring him back. By now, his chest was a patchwork of searing burn marks. Two hours had elapsed since the process had started. The room was hot and stank of sweat. The windows and patio doors had been opened, to let in the crisp night air. Outside there was nothing visible to the human eye save a sheet of deep impenetrable darkness. A mile from the vast Cairngorm mountain range, nestled in the woods, there were no street lights, no illumination from neighbours' houses, no civilisation for twenty miles. There was nothing. They were alone in the wilderness. Peter Grant was right. No one could hear you scream.

"We're having a break," said Grant, who by now had removed his pullover, and was wearing a pale-cream polo shirt daubed in sweat. Black had again dipped into unconsciousness, his head slumped forward.

"Let's get something to eat. Back at it in half an hour. Badger – you and Jack keep an eye on our friend. And Badger – you do not touch a hair on his head. Not one fucking hair. You understand this?"

Badger nodded vigorously. "No problem, Mr Grant. He's in safe hands."

"He'd fucking better be. We'll be back soon."

Grant, his five henchmen, and Nathan filed out the room. Nathan glanced back, at the dismal figure of Black, bound and broken. No one was going to win. Black was the type of man who would rather die than talk.

61

Black stirred, raised his head a fraction. The pain was general, affecting his whole body. He was given a little succour, the French doors being open, allowing in the chill night air, bringing with it a cool, soothing touch to his burnt skin. But he could still function. And he saw an opportunity.

Badger was standing three feet from him. Behind him, sitting on a long settee, was the policeman Jack Lomond, legs sprawled, slurping a bottle of beer, round face gleaming with sweat.

Black swallowed, mumbled something.

"What the fuck are you trying to say?" Badger shouted, scowling. He was holding a knife by the hilt, tapping the flat side of the blade against the palm of his other hand. It looked like a combat knife, possibly custom-made, with a serrated edge, about eight inches long. Not unlike standard US Marine Corps issue.

"Sorry about your friend with the one eye," croaked Black. "Didn't think he was your type. Thought you preferred little boys."

Badger stared at him, face crimson with anger. "What the fuck did you just say!"

"Or maybe it's the really fat, ugly type you prefer. Like Sissy Boy behind you."

Badger took one long stride forward, leaned in close to Black, pressing the tip of the knife into Black's cheek.

"Say one more word – please – and I swear, as God is my witness, I will put this blade through your mouth and slit your fucking tongue in half."

Black responded with a ghastly smile. "Or maybe rent boys. Is that what you like? Rent boys, you ugly fuck?"

Badger pressed his face up closer, almost touching. "I'm going to gut you, Black. I'll make you squeal like a fucking pig."

Close enough.

It was all Black needed.

Black snapped his mouth forward, biting deep into Badger's neck. He felt his teeth sink through skin, veins, and then the sudden burst of sticky, warm blood, as he tore through a carotid artery. He clamped his jaws tight, Badger unable to wrench himself away. Badger tried to scream, but the sound was a gurgling rattle. He waved the knife randomly, feebly. He was in shock, and convulsing, blood spraying from his neck like a fountain.

Lomond gaped, slack-jawed. He scrambled to his feet, bottle dropped on the floor, rushed over. Instantly he was spattered with Badger's blood. He tried to pull Badger off. He punched Black on the face, the side of the head. Black held him tight, like a limpet, jaws locked, teeth deep. A short struggle ensued. Jack tore Badger away. Badger clutched his throat, trying to staunch the flow of blood, his neck in shreds, blood spurting, strips of skin dangling. The chair Black was sitting on toppled over. Badger staggered, and fell sideways into the fire. In a second, his pullover was in flames.

Lomond stepped back, eyes wide, shocked at the dramatic turn of events. Badger struggled to his feet, upper body consumed in flame. He tottered across the room, banging into seats and tables. A cushion caught fire, then an entire couch and in a matter of seconds the fire had leapt to other furniture. Badger got to the open doors at the back of the room, collapsed on his knees, where he remained, his body aflame. The drapes, bunched to one side, became a sudden column of fire, springing up to the ceiling.

Lomond came to his senses. He darted out of the room. Black had maybe less than thirty seconds. Badger had dropped his knife. It was a foot from where Black lay, on his side, still strapped to the chair. Using his body, he bounced and shuffled the chair closer until he was able to grasp the hilt of the knife. Manoeuvring his hands, he began to saw the rope with the serrated edge. It was awkward, his wrists straining at the angle.

The fire was ferocious, the ceiling immersed in crackling flame, bulbs exploding, flames licking the walls. If he wasn't burned to death, then the smoke would kill him, or he would breathe in the hot air and burn from the inside.

He sawed, back and forth, muscles aching; the rope loosened, then split. His hands were free! He used the knife to cut the rope at his ankles. He kicked away the chair, and stood, gasping. A door opened – the same door Lomond had exited. There was Peter Grant, the fire forcing him back, preventing him from entering the room. For a second, their eyes locked. Black pointed the knife at him.

"Come and get me, Grant!"

Black turned away. He had to move quickly. He dodged past burning couches and tables. The grand piano was an unrecognisable lump of burning wood. He reached the open French doors and disappeared into the night. He glanced back, and glimpsed Grant staring after him, face etched in disbelief.

62

The room on fire was part of an outbuilding – the guest house, as Grant liked to describe it – set a hundred yards from the main house. Grant, Nathan and the others had no choice but to evacuate and watch as the entire building went up in flames. Nathan had never seen something catch fire so quickly.

"What the fuck happened in there!" screamed Grant.

Lomond's eyes darted left to right, glittering in the firelight. Suddenly, his flat, round features were animated. "He ripped Badger's throat open. I swear, Mr Grant. I've never seen anything like it."

"Haven't you." Grant snapped his fingers and pointed at one of his men. "Give me that." The man was holding a Luger semi-automatic pistol. He handed it to Grant. Grant aimed, and shot DS Lomond through the forehead. His head seemed to implode. The impact lifted him off his feet; he fell on his back on the grass.

Grant stood over him and fired three more shots into his face. "Fucking moron." He turned to the others. "We've got to find him. Now. He's on his own, he's freezing, and he's in pain.

He can't get far. We'll get the hunting rifles from the lodge, and torches. We'll get the bastard, no problem. But I need him alive!"

Nathan wanted to speak out, to object. Wait until morning. Bring more men up, from Glasgow. Get hunting hounds. But his uncle was not to be crossed. His uncle was in a mad-dog rage. If he opened his mouth, he would die. But then he might die anyway, on this cold winter's night in the Scottish Highlands. There were eight armed men going after one man with a knife. Nathan had a dismal feeling in the pit of his stomach. Eight men weren't enough.

63

The moon was hidden by drifts of grey cloud; the air was thin and bit the lungs with every breath. The light from the burning building gave Black a brief idea of his surroundings. He was running barefooted across a lawn, glimmering with frost. It looked almost magical. Encircling it was a wall of darkness – a wood. His immediate instinct was to take cover and lose himself in the shadows. He looked back. Foremost was the fire, the flames engulfing the entire structure. It was an outhouse, he realised. Beyond it, the silhouette of a much larger building. The main house.

Black reached the trees and paused for breath behind the wide trunk of an oak tree. He needed time to take stock, to think. Also, he got a perfect view of the fire, and the surrounding garden. His feet were already freezing. The cold bit into the raw burn marks on his chest. He was naked from the waist up, in what felt like sub-zero temperature. If he didn't get warm soon, hypothermia would set in, his pulse would slow, he would lose his self-awareness, and drift asleep. He would be dead within the hour. He needed warm clothes. And he needed a better weapon.

Emerging into the light came the men. They stood in front of the fire, so that Black could only discern outlines. But he recognised the figure of Peter Grant. Grant was shouting, probably barking out orders. He saw Grant take a gun and shoot another man, at point-blank range, and then shoot him again while he was on the ground. *There goes DS Jack Lomond. Cop. Ex-cop. Careless with his prisoner*, thought Black. And if you're careless in Peter Grant's world, you pay with your life. And it seemed Peter Grant didn't care who he killed.

They retreated, back to the big house. Black started to shiver. The adrenaline rush of the escape and then the flight was wearing off. His body temperature was cooling. He had to guess what his enemy would do – Grant needed him alive. And he needed him soon. If he were to escape, then Grant would assume the money would disappear. Theoretically, Black could transfer the money anywhere he wanted, via online banking. All he needed was a computer. If he got to safety, then anything was possible. This was Grant's worst nightmare, Black assumed, but even if he was captured, the clock was ticking. If the cops weren't already crawling over the offices of Wilson, Fletcher and Co. they would be soon. In the morning, the staff would turn the key to the front door, take the lift up to the first floor, enter the premises, and discover a litter of dead bodies. An early morning wake-up call. Screams, panic, horror, and then the cops. Computers seized, accounts frozen, and Grant's forty million lost forever.

The clock was ticking.

Black struggled to think, the freezing cold setting in rapidly. Grant had to find Black, no doubt. And soon. He would get sloppy in his haste and assume the obvious. That he would run. That he would look for a road, flag down a car, or look for a house, perhaps an isolated farmhouse, and seek shelter. That's how any normal person would react, after abduction and sustained torture. Get as far away as possible.

But Black wasn't a normal person.

64

The main house – the hunting lodge – was buzzing with activity. Grant and his men were equipping themselves. They each changed into outdoor clothing. Thick ski jackets, climbing boots, thermal trousers, gloves, mountain hats. Grant had an upstairs room in his house which was sealed shut by electronic lock. In the room were racks devoted to rifles and shotguns. On the walls were positioned a variety of semi-automatic handguns. Glocks, Brownings, Berettas. Boxes of bullets were stacked on a unit. A veritable arsenal. They armed themselves, each choosing a rifle and a handgun they tucked in their jacket pockets. Grant also took a flare gun. They trooped downstairs and into the kitchen, where Grant distributed heavy-duty flashlights.

Grant spoke quickly. "We fan out, walking through the wood, thirty yards apart. He can't get far. We need to catch him quick, before he freezes to death. You keep your fucking eyes open. If you see him, you do not kill him. He's not armed, so he's no threat. The woods stretch for two miles, then slope down to the loch. There's nowhere for him to go."

Grant scanned the waiting men who stood before him. "I

need him alive. I swear, if one of you kill him, then you're a dead man. I kid you not." He snapped his head round to a man standing behind him, dressed in track bottoms and T-shirt. "You will stay here. Keep an eye on things. Get blankets. When we bring Black back, we'll need to get him warm quickly."

The man nodded. "What if the fire brigade come? What will I tell them?"

Grant stared at him for a long second. "What did you just say? We are in the middle of fucking nowhere. Why the hell would the fire brigade come?"

"Sorry, Mr Grant," he stammered. "But you never know."

Suddenly Grant slapped the man across the face, his shoulders trembling, his face drawn and skull-like.

"Then tell them this!" he screamed. "Tell them Adam Black is burning my fucking world down!"

65

Black skirted round the periphery of the wood, keeping to the deep shadows of the trees. He had lost all sensation in his feet. His body shook with the intense cold; his teeth chattered. The wood appeared to form a natural boundary, surrounding Grant's country estate. It took Black adjacent to the main entrance of the house. He saw the men enter the main door.

Black waited. Fifty yards back, hidden in deep shadow, blowing air into his cupped hands, running on the spot, wrapping his arms about his chest. Cars were parked on a wide white-chipped driveway. Three Range Rovers. The place was illuminated by outside lights. A narrow road stretched into the darkness, presumably to a main road, dwarf walls on either side, lights built into the stone every twenty yards. Black looked up – the clouds had shifted, revealing fragments of a pale moon.

Black knew they wouldn't delay, and they didn't. They filed out ten minutes later, wearing winter gear, clutching rifles, the unmistakable figure of Grant at the head, dishing out commands. Black detected the tension in Grant's voice. His guess had been right. They were circling back round the house, to the woods behind. They assumed Black would be running away. They assumed wrong.

As soon as they were out of sight, Black sprinted to the front door. There was no cover, and he was in the full glare of the lights. If he was spotted by anyone looking out a window, or if there were security cameras, then he was finished. But he had to take the chance. He reached the front entrance. So far, so good.

He encountered a solid wooden door. He waited a breathless second, listening for any sound inside. Silence. He hadn't seen anyone take the trouble to lock it, which meant they weren't expecting Black to show, and maybe they'd left someone to watch. He turned the handle gently, pushed – the door opened, just enough to slither through – he closed it silently behind.

Immediately, he experienced warmth – a welcome sensation. He was in a wide, high hallway, deep white carpet under his feet, rich wood-panelled walls. Similar to the décor in the guest house. Doors on either side. At the top of the hall, a set of wide stairs. Nerves taut, he crept to the foot of them. He was still carrying Badger's hunting knife. He assumed the bedrooms were on the top landing.

A door opened to his right, from the kitchen. A man stood, framed in the doorway, holding a bowl of food in his hands, dressed in tracksuit trousers and T-shirt. He stopped and gaped at Black.

"You," the man croaked.

"Me." Black threw the knife, using a spin technique. The blade buried itself into the man's chest. The man stood, motionless, staring open-mouthed at the dagger embedded in his body, hilt deep. Black followed up quickly. He leapt forward, kicked the man in the groin, drew the knife out, and stabbed him through the neck. The man collapsed into Black's arms, gurgling blood.

Black eased him to the floor. Suddenly the white carpet was

red. Black waited, nerves stretched. The noise may have attracted others. The house seemed still, unoccupied. Black raced up the stairs. He was looking for the bedrooms, any bedroom. Somewhere he might find warm clothing.

More doors. He went through the rooms, until he found what he was looking for. A large room, double bed, and along one side, a series of built-in wardrobes. In them was what he needed – warm fleece-lined trousers, shirt, pullover, and in one section, a row of coats. Black put on a black snorkel-hood parka. He found a shoe cupboard, and in it, several pairs of winter boots. Black put a pair on. Slightly tight, but Black didn't have the luxury to care.

He had no weapon, except the knife. But in the dark, when people were scared, a gun wasn't essential.

Black raced back down the stairs, past the dead man on the hall floor, and out the front door.

Time to join the hunt for the man Peter Grant hated most in the world. Adam Black.

66

Black zipped up the coat's hood over his head, rendering him unrecognisable. He jogged past the burning guest house, still fully ablaze, the roof structure fallen in on itself, the flames reaching high into the night-time sky. He got to the line of trees and plunged into the darkness.

He saw flickers of light ahead, not far away. Torch beams. Also, it was impossible not to hear them, thrashing through the undergrowth, shouting to each other, and distinct was the voice of Peter Grant, bellowing commands. Their intention was not to capture him unawares. Rather, they were like hounds hunting the fox, following their prey until it could go no further, spent and exhausted. Black moved as quickly as he could, unconcerned about the noise he was making, the sounds of his passing blending in with the general clamour.

The eight men were moving slowly in the same direction, in what appeared to be a relatively straight line. Black caught up, but kept back fifty yards, working out their position by each bobbing flashlight. He targeted the man at one end of the line, and nearest him. With the dark parka, and virtually zero natural light, he was invisible.

He increased his pace, until he was a yard behind, pulling back his hood for better vision. The man he had chosen was wearing a pale-blue ski jacket, dark woollen hat pulled over his ears. He had a torch in one hand, and a rifle slung over his shoulder. Looked like a bolt-action Winchester. A hunter's rifle. Black had to move quickly and silently. The kill had to be efficient.

He executed the manoeuvre exactly as he had been trained. Placing one hand over the man's mouth, he thrust his knife hard into the side of his neck, the collar of the ski jacket offering little resistance. The man made a faint coughing spluttering sound, and collapsed immediately, Black taking his weight, lowering him gently to the ground. Black relieved him of both torch and rifle and left him shuddering in some long grass.

Now Black was part of the line. The man across from him waved and pointed his torch in his direction.

"Any sign?"

Black shone his torch back and shook his head.

They moved slowly on. Black could hear Grant cracking out the orders from the middle of the line. "Nice and slow. He can't get past us. Keep your torches straight ahead. We'll head him off. Don't shoot him. Nowhere he can go at the foot of the hill. We'll get the fucker. No problem."

Black decided it was time. He stopped, raised his hand.

"Here!" he shouted. "Here!"

The line stopped, and seven torches trained on him. He had pulled the hood of his parka back over his head, hanging loosely so that he still had good periphery of vision, but still enough to hide his face.

"Fucking brilliant!" he heard one man shout.

"Stay there!" cried Grant.

You can bet your life on it, thought Black.

The seven men angled towards him.

Black got down on one knee. For the men approaching, it would look innocent enough, as if he were crouching down to inspect something on the ground. Instead, Black switched off his torch, positioned the rifle butt in the pocket of his firing shoulder, rested his cheek on the stock, aimed the iron sights dead against the torchlight of the first approaching man, and fired.

The shot echoed through the crisp forest air. The torch dropped suddenly to the ground. Clean hit. The other torches suddenly stopped. Black didn't, working the bolt smoothly, and firing again within two seconds, aiming directly at the next beam of light. It was twenty yards further away, but well within Black's range. Another shot cracked through the winter's chill, another torch dropped to the ground. Two men down in less than five seconds. The odds were improving.

67

"What the fuck is going on!" Grant screamed.

"It's Black!" Nathan shouted. "It's Black shooting at us!"

"Jesus. He's got a gun," another shouted.

Then another voice. "Kill the torches! Kill the fucking torches!"

Too late. A third man went down, close to Nathan. Nathan saw it happening – the bullet ripping through the man's chest, his back erupting, like a volcano spewing dollops of body parts.

The torches were extinguished, the wood falling eerily silent after the noise of gunshot. A stillness settled. Nathan had leapt to the ground and crawled up behind a tree trunk. He strained to see something, anything which might indicate Black's position. But he was looking at a tangle of darkness and shadow.

His uncle was also flat on the ground, twenty yards away.

"Can you see him?" Grant hissed.

"I can't see a fucking thing! We should head back, to safety. Regroup!"

Grant did not respond immediately. Nathan imagined his uncle's mind working furiously. He was in a dilemma. If he started a gunfight, and Black was killed, he'd lose a fortune. If he did nothing, then Black might disappear, vanish in the night – or worse, continue picking them off.

"Black!" shouted Grant. "Can you hear me?"

Nothing.

"I know you can! I only want the fucking password. You give that to me, and we all walk away from this. You go your way, I go mine. You have your life back, and we forget this. What do you say? Do we have a deal?"

A voice responded, suddenly, not from the spot Nathan thought Black was hunkered in. From somewhere behind them. Nathan jumped when he heard it.

"Then we forget the whole thing?"

"That's right, Black!"

"And I forget my wife and daughter?"

"We can't go back! We both suffered. You took my son! What the fuck did you expect?"

"Nothing. Nothing at all. You'll never get the password, Grant. Accept this. Tonight, you're going to die."

Suddenly Grant stood, rifle pointed. "Kill him! Kill the fucker!" He fired in the direction of Black's voice. His men fired, including Nathan, the sound deafening. Deep down, he knew there was no chance of hitting Black in these conditions. Four rifles unleashed volleys of bullets with no idea of where they were shooting. After ten seconds the firing stopped, and again that strange unearthly hush descended on the world.

"I think I got him!" someone shouted.

A noise, forty yards away. The sound of twigs snapping, branches breaking, footsteps trampling on sticks and hard ground. The man closest to Grant was moving. Running. A sudden beam of light appeared. He had switched on his torch.

"I hit something!"

"Stay where you are!" Grant bellowed. "Turn the fucking torch off!"

The man ignored him. Another rifle shot boomed out. Nathan heard a rustle of bushes, a groan. Then silence. The torchlight disappeared.

"Where are you?" shouted Grant.

No response.

"Shit!"

Eight down to three, thought Nathan. Who's next?

His uncle was lying flat again, rifle pointed ahead. He crawled towards Nathan, who was still crouched behind a tree, hardly daring to breathe. He got to about six feet from him, and then spoke in a rasping whisper. "We can't go back. He'll take us out when we try to get to the house. We keep going. We follow the slope, until we reach the loch shore. If we can get to the boathouse, then we can get away on *Shadow*. Once we're on the loch, we're safe."

"Unless Black gets us first."

"Keep it together, Nathan. We can't see him, he can't see us. It's not far. We do it slow and careful. Keep close behind me. And don't put your torch on."

"There's still one of our men out there."

"Fuck him. It's you and me."

Nathan nodded, despite his uncle not being able to see the gesture. Nathan tried to swallow, but his mouth was too dry. It occurred to him these might be the last moments of his life. He roused himself, started to move in a creeping gait, second by painstaking second, body braced for the life-ending impact of a bullet. His uncle was five steps ahead, crouched low, heading for the boathouse at Loch Morlich.

68

Black was unsure of Grant's next move. To turn tail and make for the safety of the big house was the obvious course of action. But Grant was fighting for his life and knew that Black had already second-guessed him. Also, there was a clear kill zone between the edge of the trees and the entrance to the house. Grant might not wish to take the risk.

Black also assumed that Grant knew the lie of the land. It was Black's guess therefore, that Grant would continue onwards, to try to shake him off, lose him in the trees, and then veer back. Plus, they would not use their torches, just as it was dangerous for Black to use his. Which meant Black could easily lose them in the darkness. Black fought a sudden rise of panic. He was so close; he could taste Grant's fear. To lose him now was not an option.

He was kneeling in the midst of a cluster of pine trees. He didn't move, listening for the slightest sound, the rustle of branches, twigs snapping, any noise indicating human presence. Overhead, he heard the hoot of an owl. To his right, the vague murmur of a stream. He reckoned he was about a quarter of a mile from the burning remnants of Grant's guest house. But here, in the thick of the woods, the flames were too distant to see, so Black had to guess his bearings. The ground was sloping. Perhaps to a road? Grant had mentioned they were close to the Cairngorms. Black had once trained up in this area, climbing the mountain known as Ben Macdui with a forty-four-pound Bergen pack strapped to his back. But his knowledge of the land was limited.

There! Away to his left, perhaps a hundred yards or so, the crack of a snapping branch. Black moved carefully forward in the direction of the sound, trying not to disturb his surroundings. The going was slow. The ground beneath him was markedly sloped, the trees thinning. The clouds shifted above – the sudden moonlight gave a wan illumination. Black saw vague shapes and outlines. Trees, branches, bushes. He was walking in a strange netherworld, full of phantoms and shadows. He kept onwards, step by delicate step, careful not to make any noise. He was a ghost.

Forty minutes later, the wood gave way to a narrow, sandy beach, beyond which was the still, black surface of a loch, flat as glass, the soft sound of its waters lapping on the sand.

He stopped at the foot of a thick tree, and hunkered down, gazing left and right. Two figures were jogging along the sand, heading for a structure built on the edge of the open water. Peter Grant!

A movement close to his side. Black spun round. A man was standing, staring at him, rifle pointed in his general direction. He was as surprised at seeing Black, as Black was seeing him. The man lifted his rifle. Instinct cut in. Black dropped onto one knee, aimed, fired all in one smooth motion, hitting the man dead centre in the stomach. The man uttered a rasping croak, clamped both hands over his guts, and toppled into the shadows.

Black was out of bullets. He tossed the rifle away.

He turned back to the two men on the beach, who had obviously heard the shot, and were sprinting towards the boathouse. Black chased after them, keeping to the cover of the thin periphery of trees.

69

Grant and Nathan got to the boathouse. It was a structure in the shape of a super-sized wooden shed, protruding at least twenty-five yards into the water, the wood painted maroon. There was a door at the side, unlocked.

"Did you hear that?" Nathan glanced behind him, towards the trees, and the source of the rifle shot.

"Of course I fucking did!" snapped Grant.

"Black might be shot."

"Don't count on it."

They entered the building. Grant slammed the door shut behind them, securing two bolt locks at top and bottom. He flicked a switch. The interior was suddenly illuminated by a series of strip lights fastened by brackets on the high, flat ceiling. They were standing on a narrow wooden walkway. Docked to a piling was a twenty-foot speedboat, reinforced fibreglass body, a sleek black shark. The word 'Shadow' was emblazoned in bright-white lettering on the hull. His 'fun boat' as his uncle described it. Nathan had been on board before and had never enjoyed the experience. It made him nauseous. Tonight was different. Tonight, the boat and the water were his best friends.

"You've got keys?"

"Don't worry." Grant made his way to the back of the enclosure, to a set of cupboards and shelves, containing rope, tins of paint, petrol cans, other oddments. He pulled open a drawer, and took out a metal toolbox, which he opened. In one of the compartments was a set of keys.

"Spare," he said. "For emergencies. There's enough fuel in the tank to take us where we need to go. We'll get to the main road on the other side. It's midnight, but the Osprey is open till one. We'll phone a taxi and get the fuck out of here. Then we'll see what happens next."

Nathan knew the Osprey. A pub sitting on the shore of the loch, selling cheap beer and whisky. A popular haunt for those fed up with the tourist prices of Aviemore, twenty miles down the road.

"But what does that mean – *what's next*?" Nathan said, his voice rising to almost a whine. "Black's alive. There's a bunch of dead bodies at the lodge. What do we tell the police?"

"Fuck the police! I've got the chief constable in my back pocket. We'll blame it all on Black. Fucking psycho killer on the loose."

In the raw glare of the strip light, his uncle looked ghastly – the perpetual tan seemed to have drained away; his lean face looked gaunt, his eyes sunken into his skull, his cheekbones harsh and prominent. For the first time ever, Nathan saw him as much older than he was, frail and bitter. And mad.

Grant climbed into the cockpit and started the engine. It thrummed into life. Nathan untied the mooring rope, flung it into the boat, and climbed in after him. "Let's get the fuck out of here."

70

When Black heard the bolts on the door slam shut, he had no choice. The cautious approach was no longer a viable option. There were no windows in the boathouse, as far as he could tell, no obvious places a person could fire a rifle from. He sprinted from the trees, and across the sand, past some wooden picnic tables, a metal rubbish bin.

He got to the door, just as the low drone of the motorboat engine started up. He pulled, but it was locked solid. He ran around the back, and to the other side – there! A plastic drainpipe running from ancient guttering edging the flat roof, fifteen feet high. Black gripped the pipe with both hands, its surface slick. He shinnied up, the pipe barely holding his weight. He got to the top, pulled himself over. The roof was flat, consisting of hard, black asphalt. Black crept to the far edge, overlooking the water. He squinted down; the light from the interior of the boathouse reflected off the water's surface, giving it an oily, black glimmer.

He waited, poised. This was his only chance. He sensed movement. The bow of the boat emerged from the enclosure.

Black jumped.

71

Nathan remained behind Grant as he navigated the boat out its enclosure, the exiting manoeuvre slow at the beginning. Nathan, eyes fixed stonily ahead at the dark landscape, felt he was in an endless nightmare, unable to wake up. He was in hell. Dead men everywhere. The night was not yet over.

He sensed a blur of movement, above and behind him. He whirled round. From nowhere, a figure hurtled onto the boat, landing with a hollow thud on the stern.

Black!

He landed clumsily, the boat rocking at the sudden weight.

"What the fuck!" screamed Grant, turning to look.

Black almost bounced off, but managed to grip onto a side cleat, preventing him falling into the water. He hauled himself up and onto the boat. Nathan was too stunned to react.

"Shoot the fuck!" Grant pushed hard on the throttle. The boat picked up speed instantly, skittering across the water.

The sudden acceleration caused both Nathan and Black to lose balance, Black again almost toppling into the water.

Nathan had placed his rifle on one of the cockpit seats. He

snatched it up, and pointed square at Black's chest, only six yards from him.

"Shoot him!"

Nathan nodded.

Black stared back, directly into the barrel of a bolt-action Winchester, unflinching.

Nathan felt an overwhelming sense of elation. Black was going to die. Nathan, who detested getting his hands dirty, detested any form of violence, had no trouble acting out this final scene. Still, he couldn't keep the tremble from his hands.

"Goodbye, Black."

He pulled the trigger.

72

Black could have dived into the icy waters of the loch, but he chose not to. It had come to this. He was so close to Grant, he could almost touch him. He could smell his fear. After the ordeals he had endured, the traumas inflicted upon him, to let it go was unthinkable. Impossible. So let it play out. The man he recognised as Grant's nephew – Nathan – was pointing a rifle straight at him. But the boat was moving at high speed, bouncing and lurching across the surface of the water. And it was dark. And he knew the man facing him was scared shitless.

Bring it on. Bring it fucking on.

Nathan squeezed the trigger. The rifle clicked. No crack of the gunshot. No recoil. Nothing happened.

Misfire!

Nathan lifted his head, looked at Black, the shock in Nathan's eyes easy to read. Shock turning straight to terror.

Black reacted swiftly. He lunged forward, into the cockpit, bringing his full weight onto Nathan. They both fell backwards, cannoning into Grant, who was pushed to one side, the wheel of the boat turning sharply, all three men toppling onto the seating as the boat cut to a new direction.

Black jabbed his elbow hard into Nathan's face, nose breaking with an audible snap. Nathan emitted a squeal of pain. Grant was quick and lithe. He regained his feet, found a compartment in the dashboard, and produced a small calibre .38 revolver. He turned to fire at Black. Black was on him, grabbing Grant's gun wrist, forcing it up into the air, the shot firing harmlessly into the sky. Nathan remained sprawled on the seat, dazed, blood streaming from each nostril.

Grant headbutted Black. Black kept his grip on Grant's wrist, but the blow disoriented him. Grant battered the side of Black's face with his free hand, all his boxing training coming to the fore. Black swivelled to one side in an effort to avoid the punches, and in so doing, Grant was able to bring the gun down. Black still held on, both hands on Grant's wrist. The gun wavered back and forth, as both men fought for control. Black kneed Grant in the groin. Grant gave a low groan, his finger involuntarily jerking the trigger. Another gunshot. The top of Nathan's head erupted in a sudden spurt of blood and brain.

Grant released a savage, gut-wrenching howl. For a second, his body relaxed. Black seized his chance. He slammed Grant's hand down on a side railing. The gun fell free, dropping into the water. He brought his arm up in a brutal uppercut, catching Grant under the chin. Grant's head snapped up. He staggered back onto the dashboard. Black loomed in, inflicting two jabbing punches, both connecting. He launched a right hook – Grant blocked and struck back, catching Black in the eye. Black felt he'd been struck by a sledgehammer. Grant pulled a knife from a leather sheath attached to his trouser belt. A hunting knife. Wide blade, razor-sharp edge.

He waved the knife from side to side. He suddenly thrust forward. The boat heaved. Black tried to catch Grant's wrist but had to keep hold of the railing to avoid being ditched overboard. The knife pierced his jacket, penetrating his body, below the left side of his ribcage. No instant pain. It felt like a soft punch. Grant rounded on him, stabbing down on his neck. Black blocked with a forearm, but already he could feel the warm ooze of blood flowing. Grant used his other arm to land a heavy punch on his wound. Black reeled back, tripping on Nathan's dead body, which had rolled onto the floor of the cockpit.

Grant towered over Black, knife in one hand, lips curled back, teeth bared like an animal, eyes shining with madness. "I'm going to cut your fucking heart out!"

Then the world turned inside out, and the sky crashed into the earth, and Black slipped into darkness.

73

I'll never pause again, never stand still,
Till either death hath closed these eyes of mine,
Or fortune given me measure of revenge.
Henry VI
William Shakespeare

The sound came first. Jarringly loud. A heavy drone, constant. Like an insect was buzzing in his head. It filled Black's ears, his brain. His universe. He tried to open his eyes but couldn't. Every fibre of his body ached. His brain felt like it was going to explode.

I'm dead, he thought. But he was too sore to be dead. *Unless there was pain after death.* He tried to move, but his body resisted. The sound persisted, too intrusive to allow him to slip into unconsciousness. Gradually, his senses returned. He opened one eye. The world wavered. He was on his back, looking at the sky. It was dark, but the clouds had cleared, and he saw a million twinkling dots.

His side burnt like hell. He remembered. He'd been stabbed. By Grant. Black felt the side of his jacket. It was wet and sticky with blood.

He turned his head, towards the direction of the sound. There, ten yards away, was the speedboat. It was lying half in, half out the water, the front smashed against a pile of massive boulders. *It's run aground,* thought Black. Collided full tilt into rock, at speed. There was little left of it. A wrecked burning hulk, barely recognisable as the sleek speedboat before, flames licking the night sky. Around him, peppering the ground, shards of fibreglass, twisted metal, chunks of wood. The only section intact was the tail end of the stern, and the propeller. It was the propeller making the sound, still spinning at full power, spitting and churning up water.

He must have been flung from the wreckage. He was on soft sand. He raised himself up on one elbow. He was on a narrow strip of shoreline. Beyond was the gloom of the loch. He squinted round. Behind, more darkness. He tried to take a deep breath, but the act was painful. He suspected he had broken ribs. And he knew he was leaking blood. If he didn't get help soon, his blood would drain out, and he would die.

A thought crept into his mind. Where was Grant? A shadow flickered. A figure rose up from the wreckage, a silhouette against the flames. It came stumbling towards him. Black tried to focus, concentrate, but the world kept moving. The figure reached him, looked down, regarding Black for several seconds, as if contemplating. It was Grant, face slick with blood from a deep gash in his head, ski jacket ripped. In the red and orange glare of the burning boat, and on that lonely beach, he cut a nightmarish figure.

Behind him, the low drone of the propeller, the blades ploughing up water.

"Why don't you just fucking die, Black." Grant dropped,

suddenly straddling Black, knees pinning his shoulders onto the ground.

Black tried to resist, but Grant's body was too heavy. It was like trying to shift concrete.

"No one fucks with me," mumbled Grant. "No one." With heavy, slow fists, he pulverised Black, hard and unremitting, concentrating on his face – nose, teeth, cheeks, eyes.

Black was slipping away. Into the darkness. Oblivion. If the blows didn't kill him, the knife wound would.

One single dismal thought consumed his mind like a dark cloud – he was going to die, and Grant would win. His wife and daughter murdered, him dead, and Grant victorious.

Fuck this! His two arms were still free. He groped in the sand, searching for anything. There! A lump of metal, the size of a fist. Black grabbed it. Summoning up what little energy remained, he swung his arm up and round, striking Grant with force. Grant grunted, rolled off, clutching his head. Black began to crawl away on his stomach, in no particular direction. He saw something lying on the sand close to him and shuffled his way towards it.

If he could reach what he thought it was, the odds became considerably more favourable.

He heard movement behind him.

"You can't get away, Black!"

He heard the scrape of feet dragging across the sand, as Grant staggered towards him. He felt two hands on the back of his shoulders, as he was hauled up and flipped over.

Black gave a ghastly smile. "Time to see the light."

Grant stared slack-jawed at the snub barrel of a flare gun. He turned to get away. Too late. Black fired. The space between Black and Grant was suddenly ablaze. Grant reeled back, clawing at his face. His screams rang out across the loch, high and shrill. He weaved across the beach, towards the boat, scraping at the flames on his skin. He sank to his knees, as if in prayer, pulling the remains of his jacket up and over his head, rocking back and forth, his screams diminished to low moans, barely audible above the drone of the propeller.

Somehow, Black got up. His head pounded, his cracked ribs sent spasms of pain with each breath. He was losing blood fast, and he was burning up. The world was spinning. Still, he found his feet, and made his slow way over to Grant.

Grant knelt before him, hidden under his jacket. Black ripped it off. The face which looked up was no longer recognisable as Peter Grant. It was no longer a face, in any conventional sense – it had melted into a canvas of colour; black burnt flesh; white bone where skin had dripped away; patches of red smooth skull where hair had once been; an empty eye socket.

He mumbled something. "Help me."

"One more thing to do," said Black.

With some effort, he gripped Grant under each arm, hauled him up, dragged him along the sand, to the rear end of the boat. To the propellers. Grant offered little resistance. He spoke, his lips worked, but the words were incoherent.

Black pulled him into the freezing water, and forced him on his knees, a foot away from the spinning propeller, the blades a blur of movement as they furrowed through the water, soaking them both. Black welcomed the cold, soothing the burning agony of his body. He leant down and whispered in Grant's ear.

"Compliments of Jennifer and Merryn."

He placed the crook of his arm under Grant's chin, his other hand on the back of his head. He pushed forward. Grant tried to lean back, fighting against the pressure. But his effort was weak. Black pushed him, inch by inch, closer to the blades.

Grant struggled. Black pushed on.

The top of Grant's head brushed the propeller blades. Blood

and bone and brain scattered up into the air. Grant shrieked. Black pushed on. The blades sheared through his skull, slicing piece after piece. Black kept pushing. The shrieking stopped. Black released him and allowed Grant's body to drift away into the darkness of the loch.

Black sat down in the water. The pain had almost disappeared, now a distant sensation, a vague fuzzy numbness. A bonus, he thought.

He stretched back and floated on the still loch waters. He wondered if perhaps he should let go and join Grant on that dark journey. He was so tired. Weary down to the core of his bones. To his soul.

The water no longer felt cold. He was taking a warm bath. He looked again up at the sky. The stars remained constant, while men beneath them battled and died and then repeated the same thing, again and again, endlessly.

He remembered the blood moon, how it glistened red in the sky when the whole saga began.

Then he remembered something else. Something important.

There was one more thing to do.

Adam Black somehow struggled to his feet and made his way to the shore.

74

ONE YEAR LATER

The Rue des Martyrs. A street in Paris. Not as grand as some, but quaint and whimsical, lively and colourful. Filled to the brim with coffee shops and patisseries; jewellery shops offering handcrafted designs. Bistros and bookshops; glossy red buildings advertising cabaret; eccentric little restaurants; butchers and bakers selling local produce under brightly-coloured awnings. Buskers played music, from Chopin to Led Zeppelin. Tables and chairs lined the pavements where people sat and chatted and smoked, or sat alone, reading a newspaper or a book. Or just sat, absorbing the colour, the energy, the buzz. It was summer, and the Paris streets were hot. The Rue des Martyrs was busy and bustling.

At a table in the shade sat one such man, alone. He wasn't reading. He seemed to be doing nothing in particular, other than enjoying watching the passing crowd, a small cup of espresso on the glass-topped table in front of him. A man easily forgettable. Nondescript, pale, almost sallow, bland features. Balding. Wearing dark flannels, dark jacket, white shirt, open at the collar. Innocent and unassuming. A man who blended in.

He took a sip of his coffee, gazing round at the other people sitting near him. One individual caught his attention. A man sitting at a corner table, at the opposite end of the café, alone like himself. A vague hint of recollection teased his mind. A prick of uneasiness disturbed him. He ignored it and took another sip. He looked again. The man was staring at him. Unnervingly so. Insultingly so, he thought. A hard-looking individual, dark-haired, chisel-featured, square-jawed. The man was drinking a similar cup of espresso, which he raised, nodding at him.

How could he know this man? It didn't seem likely. Suddenly he felt ill at ease. His agitation intensified when the man rose from his seat with his coffee cup and saucer in hand, weaved his way through the maze of furniture, to stand at the other side of his table.

"Do you mind if I join you?"

He shrugged, uncomfortable. But intrigued.

"I'm just about to go, actually."

"I'll take that as a yes."

The man sat. He was big, possibly six-two, well-muscled, and moved with the innate sureness of an athlete.

"We've never met," said this man. "But I know you."

"Really? I can't recall."

"Possibly not. You might remember my family better."

He raised an eyebrow. "I'm not sure I follow."

"You visited them once. At my house. You murdered them. You shot them both in the head. You killed my wife Jennifer in the kitchen. Then you killed Merryn, who was four years old, as she was watching television. Then you left. I think I've got that right."

He listened. Suddenly the gloss and excitement of the busy street vanished. He sat, still, unmoving. He licked his lips, trying to conceal his nervousness.

"I think you're mistaken."

"I don't think so, Joshua. When it comes to hunting scumbags, I'm rarely wrong. And I've tracked you down to this café. You're a hard man to find. But I've been watching you for some time now. And here we are."

Joshua swallowed, composed himself. He was not a man to be taken by surprise. But here he was.

"I'm afraid you have a fanciful imagination," he said. "Perhaps you should seek medical advice, my friend. If you don't be careful, I'll shout for a gendarme."

"Please, be my guest. We would have an interesting conversation."

"I'm sorry but I think you have... how shall I say... an overactive imagination."

"Perhaps. But I'm going to kill you, regardless."

It was time to go, Joshua decided. Now. He stood, dropping some coins on the table. "I wish you luck in your endeavours. But I really think you need help. What did you say your name was?"

"My name? Adam Black. Don't forget it."

THE END

Printed in Great Britain
by Amazon